ONE DARK NIGHT

One Dark Night

A Ravenquill Anthology

Steam Engine Productions

Contents

The Ravenquills   vi

1   Who Killed Granny?   1

2   Arachne   29

3   I'm Innocent   51

4   Painting the Dead   70

5   Space Silk   95

6   The Egg House   115

7   The Professor's Death   134

8   The Lodemirror Estate   155

The Ravenquills

Legend says this group started years ago at some nameless writers conference. A handful of aspiring Young Adult/SciFi authors sat around a lunch table chatting about their writing hopes and dreams. One turned to the other and said, "Want to start a writers group?" And the Ravenquills were born. Over the years this group has grown and changed, but with each new writer, new inspiration is born.

The Ravenquills are a group of women who love the craft of writing fiercely and help lift one another through weekly meetings and chapter critiques. They aren't afraid to ask questions or muse about how many firearms a woman could possibly hide on her person while running for her life from a giant moth creature on a swamp planet. (The answer is seven, by the way.) These stories are but a small sampling of the incredible talent in this group. Enjoy!

1

Who Killed Granny?

J. ANN CURTIS

My boyfriend, Warren, placed the black curtains he'd torn from the window over Granny's mangled body. I'd been standing there for almost a full ten minutes. Just staring. A scream lodged in my throat.

No two ways about it, Granny was dead.

Murdered.

Her gnarled hand stuck out from under her dark covering, curled against the wooden floor of her office. Her antique desk, with papers strewn across it, sat at the far end of the room. Had she tried to escape? Little good it had done her.

I shouldn't have allowed her to stay late—should've insisted that she come home. She would have listened to me. I should've stayed by her side with my crossbow locked and loaded.

"Red?" Warren's warm hands ran over my arms, his brilliant blue eyes a sea of concern. "What can I do?"

What do you do when your world has been demolished in one morning?

Granny's no-nonsense words resounded inside my head. *You soldier on. That's all there is to do for our kind, Red.*

Even though it wouldn't have saved her, I wished I hadn't overslept that morning. I never slept in. But that day, while my grandmother's mangled body grew cold in her office, I was peacefully resting in Warren's arms.

I swallowed back the pain, stiffening.

"Someone will need to contact Darion Mace." My voice sounded rough and scratchy even to my own ears. "He's the next in line to lead the hunters after Granny."

"You know who did this," Warren said. "You know what Darion will do."

I took in the bloody paw prints stained across the wooden floor and recalled the deep teeth marks along Granny's skin. I shivered.

Werewolves.

But it didn't make sense. Killing Granny was an act of war. My jaw clenched, my fingers drawing into fists. She'd spent so much time establishing peace between us and our lycanthrope neighbors. Why now? They weren't dumb. Kallias had risen as their new alpha within the last year, but he seemed content with running things the way his father had. I'd never met the wolfish leader, but Granny always spoke of him with respect.

I wasn't going to let her death mark the end of all she'd worked for.

That didn't mean the culprit would get off the hook. Far from it. I was going to find the scumbag and make them pay.

"I'll go talk to the wolves." Turning, I stalked from the room into the front area that housed our weapons.

Crossbows, knives, and guns hung from pegs on the wall. For a moment, I just looked at them. Granny's bow had been sitting, unfired, next to her desk where she always kept it. Whoever attacked her had taken her by surprise. I mechanically took down a crossbow and a case of bolts. The hunter's weapon of choice. Silver bullets were rarer and, when it came to retrieval, messier.

Warren followed me. "I'll go with you." He pulled the dark-blue windbreaker he wore everywhere from the coat rack and shrugged his broad shoulders into it.

I jerked my cloak from the same rickety wooden rack and threw it on. "No, I need you to make sure everything goes well here. Watch over her"—I gulped—"body. If this gets out before we can set up a meeting with Darion, there will be panic."

"And I don't want to find you dead," Warren shot back, that protective side that was both endearing and aggravating showing through. "At least take some others with you."

The last thing I wished to do was start a war by dragging a load of hunters into wolf territory. Yet.

But I couldn't fault Warren for worrying, even though I felt like burning the entire world to the ground. "I'll take Lexa."

* * *

"Are you sure you're up for this, Red?" Lexa, my best friend, treaded at my side, wearing a matching forest-green cloak. "It hasn't been twenty-four hours. Hell, it was only a few hours ago that you found her. If it were me, I'd be a blubbering—"

"I'm fine." I stalked ahead, clenching my teeth. Moving. *Just keep moving. I'll figure this out.*

Lexa flipped her long, dark braid over her shoulder. "Well, if you need to talk—"

"I said I'm fine."

She narrowed her mahogany eyes. With her brown skin and elegant figure, Lexa was a beauty. With my freckles, fiery hair, and pale skin—well, at least I was brave. She fingered the crossbow in her hands. "These wolves better be on their best behavior."

"We only want to speak with them." The dirt road crinkled beneath my feet, and the wooden structures of the village loomed on either side of us. I kept my gaze steady on the not-too-distant tree line, a harsh wind whipping my cloak around my body.

She glanced at me. "This is dangerous, Red. If they are willing to kill our leader—"

"We don't know that for sure," I said quietly.

That was what we'd come to figure out.

We left the boundary that marked our small town and headed into the darkness of the woods.

Lexa's eyes darted about. She was on her guard. Good. If my blood weren't up, perhaps I'd share more in her caution. Nothing but determination drove me forward. That single-mindedness cleared my body of all other sensations.

The greenery of the forest snagged our cloaks, and the occasional chirping of birds and skittering of small animals sounded through the brush. The air felt fresh and was pungent after a recent rain. Silence enveloped the surrounding forest the moment we crossed into wolf territory, and a heavy mist blanketed the ground, clinging to our ankles.

A flash of huge teeth and the rumble of threatening growls signaled we had found the wolves. Their forms moved through the bushes. Sleek and agile. Their powerful bodies are strong enough to take down either of us in an instant.

They encircled us, hazy specters in the mist, cutting off any path of retreat.

Lexa raised her crossbow, sweat gathering on her forehead.

"It's okay. This is what we came for," I reminded her. "Don't do anything hasty."

I couldn't believe I was reassuring her. After everything that had happened, I should be the twitchy one, but I felt no danger, only a blazing desire to sort this out.

"Where is your alpha?" I asked.

The wolves moved in, bringing their circle of death even tighter. They rose nearly to my chest. A brutish wolf with rough brown fur, a sizeable chunk out of the right ear, and a scar across his snout approached, a low growl in his throat. Despite the obvious threat, an unexpected calm washed through me, and I knew he had no intention of hurting us. It made little sense.

"Red! Watch out!" Lexa pointed her crossbow at the wolf that was inches from me.

"No, wait!" I shouted.

I flinched as the twang of release sounded. The bolt buried itself in the wolf's side. He released a yelp and tumbled to the earth, crimson blooming across his shaggy coat.

An enormous, beautiful black wolf lunged from the forest. Larger than any I had ever seen. The top of his head reached my chin. He stared me down with yellow eyes and a stance that dared me to challenge him. I didn't need to ask. This was clearly Alpha Kallias. He stood over the whimpering injured wolf, glowering at us, teeth bared, deadly rage in his gaze.

Snarls tore from the wolves surrounding our position. I spun as they lunged for Lexa, stupidly turning my back on the furious wolf, who could kill me in an instant. Teeth sank into Lexa's cloak, yanking her to the ground.

"No, stop! Don't hurt her!" I raised my crossbow, prepared to fire to protect my friend.

The wolves backed off, though one snagged Lexa's crossbow and dragged it with him. My chest fluttered with surprise and relief. They had actually listened.

But they didn't seem happy about it. The lethal creatures returned to circling and growling.

"Who are you?"

I turned to where the large black wolf had been. In his place stood a tall, shirtless man. His dark hair was loose and hung to his shoulders; ebony pants covered his bottom half. He glared at me with anger in his amber eyes. The same eyes I'd been staring into a moment before when he'd been in wolf form. Kallias.

The crossbow was slick in my sweaty hands. "I'm Red. I've come to find a killer."

He stepped closer, eyes narrowing. "And yet you attack my wolves?"

I squared my shoulders. "My companion got jumpy when your wolf nearly attacked me."

He looked at Lexa, who scrambled to her feet. She stood next to me, her face unusually pale.

Kallias turned to address the pack. "Vera, see to Raedon."

A sleek white wolf transformed into a lovely woman wearing black pants and a tank top. Her eyes matched Kallias's. She moved forward and examined the injured one. "It hit him in the shoulder." She reached a hand around the shaft and pulled it out.

The wolf let out a sharp yelp, then settled into stillness. She hissed at the bloody, silver-tipped bolt and tossed it aside. "He will need time to heal, but he'll live." She motioned to a couple of other wolves. "We will take him to the den."

Kallias laid a hand on Vera's shoulder before turning to me and Lexa. "I should kill her for trespassing on my land and attacking my kin." He lifted his chin toward Lexa, though his eyes flashed over me.

Apparently, Lexa wasn't worth addressing.

"If you kill another hunter, you will have a war on your hands," I said, scowling at him.

"Another hunter? Careful of your accusations, human." He pressed closer and released a low growl that rumbled deep in his throat. "And what wolf have you killed lately?"

My heart raced. His woodsy scent surrounded me, and even though I should have been scared, I wanted to lean into him. For a moment, I struggled to breathe. I'd never experienced such a powerful pull from anyone. I wanted to run my hands over his raging hot skin, to feel his silky hair between my fingertips.

With effort, I tore my eyes away from his. He was doing something to me. Something unnatural. I took a slow, steadying breath and forced myself to step back.

Kallias was the enemy.

"I've no idea what you mean," I said. "Someone murdered my granny, our leader, in cold blood."

His fists balled. "And you assume it was the wolves?"

"There were . . . signs." I tried to shove the memory of finding Granny's mutilated body aside, but a tremor ran from my head to my toes.

He observed me, his form stiff, but his face relaxed a little. "I'm sorry for your loss," he said softly. "It's difficult to lose a loved one so close to you."

His tone spoke of someone who could relate to my pain. It struck me deep inside. A stinging started behind my eyes. Kallias's father had died only last year. He understood what it was to lose the person who was both family and leader.

I angrily reached up and swiped at my eyes. Lexa stood silently beside me, probably grateful that nobody had followed through on their death threat. I shoved my emotions aside and focused on the man in front of me.

"We had an agreement, your granny and the wolves," Kallias said. "Whoever killed her was no friend to us."

I drew the edges of my cloak tighter around me. "If the killer isn't found, our new order leader, Darion, may declare war."

But the killer *would* be found. I'd see to that. Both to avenge Granny and to honor her legacy.

Kallias pressed his lips tight and ran his palm over his sculpted chest in thought. "I'll question my pack, and if I find the one responsible among us, I'll turn them over to you. It is the only way to keep the peace. Return in two days."

"Thank you," I said and turned to Lexa. "Let's go."

He caught my arm through my cloak, forcing me to face him. Distrust speared through me, and my finger twitched on my crossbow.

"Beware, Red," he said in a low voice. "There is a killer on the loose, and it may not be who you think it is."

I gazed up into his handsome face, noting the crease between his eyebrows, the way his lips pulled down, his intense stare. It tugged at me again, the desire to be close to him. Did wolves have some weird compulsion power I didn't know about? He wouldn't trick me into believing he was innocent. I eased from his grasp, the heat in my blood causing my voice to shake. "They will regret the day they messed with my family."

His frown only deepened as I moved to join my friend and we began our return to town. We walked down the main street of our small community that was surrounded by forest on every side. villagers bustled about in their daily lives. Hunters protected these people. We weren't supernatural so much as well trained to keep the paranormal, like wolves and other dark creatures, from hurting them.

Lexa walked with me, her chin tucked. "Thanks for defending me. I . . . I messed up."

"Don't worry about it."

"Why did they listen to you, do you think?"

"What?"

"The wolves. When you told them to leave me alone, they did."

I shrugged. "Perhaps Kallias signaled for them to back off?"

"Maybe." She chewed on her lip for a moment. "He seemed a bit . . . protective of you."

My heart burned at her words, but I shook my head. "He doesn't want to be the one to start a war."

"Which makes him an unlikely culprit."

It was true. I was unsure why Kallias listened to me and agreed to back off where Lexa was concerned, or why he acted as if he cared what happened to me. But I didn't trust myself around him. My responses were too strong when I was near him. What did we really understand about the capabilities of our dangerous canine neighbors?

"I gotta help my dad with the pharmacy. But your granny already paid for her next dose of medication," Lexa said, her face scrunching with sympathy. "I'll get the money to you soon. It isn't fair to keep." I looked at her, bewildered. "Granny didn't take any medicine."

Lexa swore softly. "I forgot you didn't know." She ran a hand over her face. "Warren is going to kill me."

That wasn't right. Medication was very scarce and expensive, and Granny had always refused to take any that might otherwise serve the people of the town.

"Warren knew?"

She gave me a sheepish look. "He's been picking it up for her because he thought you'd worry about the cost."

"It's okay." Dread curled inside my gut like a predator ready to overwhelm me at any moment. There was so much I didn't know. So many unanswered questions. And now Warren was adding to them.

A few hours later, I sat with my boyfriend in our small apartment above the baker's shop. The scent of freshly baked bread constantly permeated our tiny living space. Granny had lived in the room next to ours. I'd spent the afternoon combing through her things, and found the blood pressure medication Lexa had spoken of. I'd stashed it in my pocket, saving it for after I had explained everything that had happened with the wolves to Warren.

He leaned back in his chair at the dining table and shook his head. "After what Lexa did, I can't believe they didn't attack you."

Lifting the bottle of pills from my pocket, I dropped it onto the kitchen counter. I bit my lip and glared at him. He looked concerned, but could I trust him? Could I trust anyone?

"Lexa says you've been picking up medication for Granny?" I asked.

He frowned at the pills, sliding a hand through his sandy hair. "I've been getting blood pressure medication for your granny for the past few months. She didn't want anyone else to know." He glanced up at me, apologetic. "Especially you."

Betrayal slammed through me. At Granny, who assumed I couldn't handle her frailty, but also at Warren. Suspicion burned through my veins. "What else have you been hiding from me?"

He blinked as if surprised. "Whoa, Red. You're overreacting." Reaching out, he took my hand in his. "I was trying to help."

I shut my eyes, willing myself away from the emotional brink on which I teetered. What was I thinking? Blaming him for hiding Granny's medical condition didn't mean he had anything to do with her death.

"You should have told me."

His head dipped in a nod. "I'm sorry. I think your granny didn't want to destroy that vision you've always had of her as this strong, non-compromising hero."

He ran a hand up my arm, and I sank into his touch, letting his warmth surround me as he tugged me into his lap. Warren had been with me all last night, lying in our bed, with his safe, strong arms encircling me, just like this.

"I'm here for you, Red."

"I'm sorry," I murmured.

He sighed. "There is something else. Darion wants to talk to you tomorrow to see how your meeting went. Honestly, finding the killer may not be enough for him. He seems hell-bent on declaring war."

My stomach dropped. "I'll head over to speak with him first thing."

Warren gave me a cautious glance. "He, uh, has taken up residency in your grandmother's office."

I leapt from his arms. "Has he no respect?"

"I'm sure he does. He just needs to be seen as leading from a place of power. We can't be showing our enemies that we give any ground."

With a sigh, I slumped into him. "I suppose."

Darion was always more bloodthirsty than Granny. He'd been itching to go after the wolves for years. Still, it was ridiculous to suspect him. And yet, that is exactly what prodded at the back of my mind.

The next day, I was up with the dawn, throwing on my clothes and downing a cup of donuts and coffee. My elbow knocked a few old photos off the counter, and I bent to pick them up.

The first was a picture of Warren's family beaming up at me with welcoming smiles. I'd never met them, but I hoped to one day. Though, Granny's funeral probably wasn't the right time. He, his parents, and two younger brothers were gathered around a large open-hearth fireplace, looking like the epitome of serenity. An ache of envy started in my chest. Most of my family was gone. I flipped to the next photo of my Aunt Val. Her broad smile stretched across her face, igniting a painful reminder that I needed to send her, my last remaining relative, word about Granny's death.

I'd do that later today.

The last image was of those who had founded the village many years ago when I was only three. Darion Mace stood there, bold as brass, as if he were going off to war, his son, Irvin, on his shoulders. Granny stood at the center in all her glory, smiling with a crossbow clutched between her palms. At her side stood my parents, beaming up at me. They'd been dead so long I hardly remembered them. Mother, with fiery hair that matched mine exactly, held toddler-Red in her arms. My throat tightened, and I was about to flip to the next photo when something caught my attention. A boy lingering on the edge of those gathered. He had black hair that fell to his shoulders, and he possessed an expression I recognized.

What was Kallias doing at the founding of our village?

Warren groaned and squinted from the bed, the warm rays of the sun glinting off his messed shaggy hair. "What are you doing at this ungodly hour?"

I shoved the photos onto the counter and grabbed my shoes from under the mattress, my heart beating fast. "Going to see Darion."

"Can't we get a few more hours of rest—"

"No."

He let out another groan. "Okay, just a moment. Let me get dressed."

I straightened my back, taking a calming breath. "You don't have to come."

He looked at me, his gaze piercing right through me. "You think you are okay, but I know you better, Red." He rose, grabbing his shirt off a nearby chair. "No shooting Darion when he says something you don't like. And he *will* say something you don't like."

I picked up my crossbow, grumbling. "Yeah, whatever."

As we walked back to Granny's office, I couldn't help but recall how the day before I'd found her there, lying on the wood floor, shredded and unmoving, bite marks along her body, huge chunks of flesh missing. Nausea rolled over me, and I forced my thoughts to stop.

The village was barely waking. Those who rose with the sun shuffled about setting up shop, seeing to livestock, and putting the first breads on the fire. This life is all they had left after the paranormals launched a coordinated attack and ran rampant through their world. I was merely a baby when that happened. Now they were fortunate to have simple things like electricity a few hours a day. I was lucky. I lived above the baker's shop and had a generator to run my coffee maker in the morning.

"Behold! The ones of the night shall reign down judgment upon these people unless we turn unto them!" Ezekiel Ranster brushed his stringy hair from his face and gazed around with wild eyes. He stood in front of his small, rickety home with a couple of other followers, shouting at those who passed by. "Do we not see that those powerful wolfish creatures on our border deserve our adulation?"

I sighed.

Warren cast a side glance at me. "Looks like the Night Worshippers are out early today."

Ezekial raised his arms, his beady eyes locking onto me as we passed. "I say to you, let us throw off the burdensome yoke of our hunter overlords and embrace the transcendent for the gods and goddesses they are!"

Warren snorted and wagged his head. "Poor deluded fool."

Ezekiel and his followers had shown up only a few months ago. He was the nephew of an older villager.

I desired to keep the peace between us and the wolves, but that didn't mean I wished to become one. Or to be at their mercy. Part of our job as hunters was to protect every human. Even the ones who needed protection from themselves.

But today, their words held a sinister aspect to them. Could these zealots, chaffing under hunter rule, have taken things into their own hands? Surely they realized it would do them no favors. Another hunter could simply step into a fallen leader's place.

I glanced back at Ezekial, noticing for the first time a bandage peeking out of his shirt between his neck and shoulder. Large enough to cover a bite. . . . His eyes met mine, and he jerked his shirt up around his neck and gave me a nasty leer.

"Are you okay, Red?" Warren asked.

I jerked my gaze away. It wasn't like interrogating Ezekial would get me anywhere. We weren't on good terms. He would refuse to answer my questions. Besides, I needed to confront Darion before he declared war on the wolves.

"Yeah, everything's fine."

We stepped into the weapons room, and immediately my pulse raced. I swallowed, and my hands shook. Through the door, at the rear of the room, was Granny's office—now Darion's office.

Warren's warmth was at my side. "Steady."

I sucked in a long breath and nodded. I needed to speak with Darion, no matter what a disrespectful ass he was.

Darion's son, Irvin, stood guard outside the door, loaded down with silver-tipped bolts and a gleam in his eye that said he wanted to use them. "Ah, here she is. Finally. Waltzing up while war looms on our very doorstep."

"Stop, Irvin." Warren's jaw clenched. "She just lost her granny."

Irvin sneered, adjusting his thin frame and looking over his long nose at us. "All the more reason she should be the one clamoring for vengeance, instead of running off to the wolves to get their so-called side of the story. After what happened, she should recognize better than anyone that they can't be trusted."

"I will defend Granny's legacy," I snarled at him.

"It doesn't matter. The decision is out of your hands. The whole thing has only been a matter of time, if you ask me. Your granny was weak, letting the wolves wander where they desired while they should be under our leash or dead." He gave me a satisfied smirk. "Dead dogs can't cause mischief."

My teeth squeezed together. Kallias had acted more compassionate than this man.

"That's low, Irvin." Warren threw back his broad shoulders. "Attacking Granny's rule before she's even in the grave."

He sniffed. "It's the truth. And I'm not afraid to say it."

Fury burned hot in my veins. Warren's calming hand brushed along my spine. "Easy, Red."

Looking down, I noticed I had pulled my crossbow off my back. I stared at it, already locked and loaded, ready to fire on Irvin. I closed my eyes briefly, then returned it, forcing myself to take deep, slow breaths. "Let's go."

We passed Irvin, entering Granny's office. A deep gash lingered in the door where it had been forced open, the sunlight blazed through the window with the missing curtain. My stomach churned at the bloodstains still apparent on the floor. A boiling started in my blood, and I had the sudden urge to pull my crossbow on Darion and demand what kind of game he was playing.

Warren may be right. I may be a bit out of control this morning.

Darion looked up from the papers on his desk and smiled.

"Come in. Come in. Let me start out, Red, by saying I am sorry for your loss."

"If you were truly sorry, you wouldn't be here, sitting in her desk the day after she's gone."

Darion's head bobbed, as if my reaction was perfectly reasonable. "Visitors need to remember the significance of what happened here yesterday. Besides, your granny always acknowledged that this space belonged to the order, not to her."

I folded my arms and glared at him, hating that he was right. Glancing over the stack of papers, my attention was drawn to the wolf's skull sitting on the corner of his desk. Darion followed my gaze with a smile curving his lips.

"You like that? I collect them, you know." He ran his fingers over the smooth bone, stroking it as if it had once been an old pet. "The skulls of all the wolves I've killed before your granny's contract. Back in my glory days."

I clenched my teeth against the shudder that tingled down my spine. The sharp canines reflected in the overhead light, and I tried not to think of similar teeth tearing into Granny. I tried not to think about Kallias.

Darion adjusted his bulky form in the small chair. "Warren told me you went to speak with the wolves yesterday."

"Yes, and they are cooperating. Kallias is checking to see if any of his wolves were involved. He was surprised to hear about . . . what happened."

"And you believe him?" Darion asked. "You're sure it wasn't an act put on for your benefit?"

I hesitated, remembering the strange reaction I had to Kallias. Still, I didn't want to give Darion any fodder against the wolves until I discovered for myself whether they were guilty. "You assume I wouldn't be able to see through his act?"

He motioned toward the paw prints on the blood-stained floor. "I'm afraid the evidence points to them. I can't let this kind of violation stand. We must remind the wolves what happens when they choose to break our contract."

I slammed a hand down on his desk. "No!"

Darion raised an eyebrow.

I pulled back, tugging on my cloak, and trying to keep my cool. "We need to be sure it was them first. Let me—give me a few days."

Darion gave me a considering look. "I am not unreasonable. There are four days 'til your granny's funeral. It would be unseemly to declare war before we give your granny the respect she deserves. You have until then to prove it was someone other than our wolfish neighbors. If not, it is war."

I returned to the forest the next day, as agreed upon. This time, instead of being met with an entire pack of wolves, Kallias was there alone. He watched me approach with his intense stare and his shirtless body that made my breath catch.

"Well? Did you find anything?" I demanded past the dryness in my throat.

"None of my wolves are to blame for your granny's death." Kallias was a bit too calm for my liking.

"And you're sure about that?"

His eyes narrowed. "Are you questioning my integrity, human?"

"A wolf performed the attack," I shot back.

He let out a low warning growl. "There are such things as rogue wolves." A spark of wind brushed the tips of his hair and across his muscled shoulders.

"Well, the hunters are going to declare war after Granny's funeral in three days, so you might want to look harder."

He released another growl, anger sparking in his amber eyes, and my blood ran cold, though I didn't know if it was fear at his reaction or trepidation at the idea that the attacker could be a rogue wolf living, unbeknownst to us, in our midst.

"If it is a rogue wolf, I'm going to need your help to find him." I possessed limited knowledge concerning werewolves, but I trusted their sense of smell.

He didn't move, staring at me as if conflicted. But then, he shrugged. "If it will clear the names of me and my pack, I will help you."

I knew right where I wanted to start.

He walked with me toward the town, each step smooth, like he was on the prowl. Kallias kept turning his head, a wary expression on his face, fists clenching and unclenching.

"So, you were here when the village was founded," I said, bringing up the information I'd gathered from the photo in my room.

He cast me a surprised glance. "Yes. A long time ago, before I was turned."

I shook my head. "That is against the contract."

His shoulders squared, a muscle in his jaw flexing, making him look all the more on edge. "This was before the contract."

"But how did you—"

"Look, I'd really rather not talk about that."

An annoyed breath seeped out of me. "Fine."

He released a low rumble from his throat, glaring at the silver-tipped weapons being forged at the blacksmith's shop as we passed.

"Don't worry," I said. "The agreement between granny and the wolves stated you could enter under the protection of the hunters."

"And you have the authority to guarantee that protection?"

I frowned, noting the suspicious glances being thrown from the townspeople. Maybe I should've made sure he wore a shirt and shoes so he wasn't so recognizable. "I guess not. But we aren't at war yet."

That seemed to settle him down a little as determination took over his actions. "Who do you wish me to sniff out first?"

"There." I pointed toward Ezekial Ranster who stood in his normal spot on the street with his two followers.

Kallias eyed him. "The closer I am, the more accurate I will be."

So, I brought him right up to Ezekial. "Hello, Ezekiel. Having a good day? Have you met Kallias?"

Ezekial's eyes grew round, and he started to shake. "Your Eminence." He fell on his face at Kallias's feet. "Your Most-High Gloriousness!"

Kallias stumbled back a step, giving me a bewildered look.

I rolled my eyes. "Get up, Ezekial. We have questions for you and your followers about my granny."

Ezekiel didn't rise, but his voice took on a vehemence. "Your granny died, and Darion will die too unless every one of us accepts our true masters." He motioned toward Kallias. "Oh, my lord, how may I be of service to you?"

"Um, carry on," was Kallias's only response. He took my arm and pulled me away.

"Oh, I shall, I shall, my lord. I shall not stop until I've converted them all to your magnanimity." He moved to follow, but Kallias held up a hand.

"No, stay. Your work is here."
"Yes, yes, my lord."

A small smile was playing at Kallias's lips as he pulled me away down the street. "That was . . . unexpected. If more people were like that, coming into town wouldn't be so bad."

I released a short breath of disbelief. "You wish. Most townspeople think you either want to turn them into wolves or rip out their throats."

"Ah yes, the brutal wolf-seeking-world-domination stereotype." His voice was laced with sarcasm.

"Because you're *actually* all just cuddle-balls of fur, right?"

His grin grew, a dark glint flashing in his eyes. "Perhaps we're something in between."

I snickered.

Something about the humor in his gaze caused a warmth to spread through my chest, even though it shouldn't have. A hint of a dimple appeared in his right cheek.

Warren's loyal, steady gaze flashed through my mind, and guilt twisted in my gut. "Well, don't expect to be welcomed with such open arms by anybody else," I snapped. "Did you find anything?"

The levity in his expression faded. "It's not him."

My hope shriveled. "He had a bandage under his shirt. I suspected a wolf had bitten him."

"If he were turning, I'd be able to smell it."

"What if he's working with someone—"

"He's clean. I didn't even get a whiff of wolf or blood that isn't his own on him. No, he hasn't been near a wolf within the last week." He gave me a curious stare. His hand still gripped my arm and the nearness of his bare skin caused my cheeks to warm.

"What is it?" I asked.

He let go, stepping away. "Nothing."

Whatever he was doing to me wouldn't work. I had a boyfriend.

"Wait, you can smell if they've even been near a wolf in the last week?" I considered my other suspects, Darion and his son. But how could I get Kallias near enough to them without starting the next wolf–hunter war? I tapped a finger on my leg in thought. Of course, there was a place I might get him near enough. "Can you come to a funeral?"

He snorted softly. "If I come to the funeral, we definitely will start a war."

I gave him a sly smile. "Not if I am the one who invites you."

He pressed his lips tight, looking skeptical.

"If it's not your wolves and it's not Ezekial, then it has to be some-one working with a rogue wolf," I pressed. "Darion and his son have directly benefited from Granny's death. It has to be one of them. Come to the funeral, and I'll give you my protection and you can get close enough to tell if it was them. Please."

"You're playing a dangerous game, Red."

"Granny deserves to have her true killer brought to justice. And it may be the only way to forestall war."

He finally nodded. "Fine. I'll come."

* * *

We held the funeral on a Wednesday at a small church on the edge of town.

Aunt Val, my last surviving family member, was there, having come from a village several days away. I'd sent a message to her the day after Granny's death. She had traveled far and fast to get there in time. I appreciated her effort. When I saw her, I almost broke down then and there. She pulled me into one of her famously tight hugs. "Well, Red. It is a sad business." She gazed at me through her black veil. "But I guess the good news is that I finally get to see you and meet this boyfriend of yours that I've heard so much about. Warren, right? Where is he?"

I looked over her shoulder, searching the woods for Kallias, who had yet to arrive. "He's already inside."

She raised an eyebrow and followed my gaze to the woods. Understanding filled her face. "Don't worry, my sweet, they wouldn't dare attack now. Not with a church full of hunters." She gave me a fierce glance.

She must have some weapons on her. Even at funerals, hunters were always ready for an attack. I'd stashed my crossbow under the church pew a few hours before anyone arrived.

My knees trembled. I might be recklessly putting Kallias in an obscene amount of danger. Perhaps this wasn't such a good idea. I gripped the black fabric of my skirts, recalling his smile that had unexpectedly warmed me. Since when did I care so much about what happened to the alpha wolf?

But from the looks of things, he must have also rethought our agreement because he was nowhere to be seen. I didn't know whether to be disappointed or relieved.

"Shall we?" Aunt Val looped her arm through mine, and I gave her a brief nod before turning and entering the church.

Darion was there with his son, sitting near the front. The small church consisted of some pews, Granny's casket, and a podium up at the front. Besides the front doors, a small side exit off to the left was the only other way out.

I led Aunt Val to our seats where Warren already waited, looking dashing in a dark suit. He held the normal lightweight windbreaker that he wore everywhere in his arms. Seeing him there released some of the tension tangled up inside me. I really was lucky to have him with me through all of this. He rose and smiled when Aunt Val and I reached our pew.

"Aunt Val, this is Warren. Warren, my aunt Val."

Aunt Val stumbled next to me, her nails sinking into my skin.

Warren extended a hand to her. "Glad to make your acquaintance. Red has told me so much about you."

"Y-yes. Good to meet you, Warren." She took the proffered hand, though her movements were stiff.

"I'm terribly sorry for your loss," he said. "Come, please. Have a seat."

We sat on the pew, and Warren settled next to me on my other side. He looked downcast. That shouldn't be surprising, it was a funeral after all.

"What is it?" I asked.

He gave me one of his fake smiles. "Oh, just thinking about Granny. I have good news, actually. Darion says he's thinking of putting off a declaration of war. He fears he's being hasty."

Hope sprang into my chest. "Really?"

Warren smiled through gritted teeth. "Really."

The doors to the church were pulled shut, and the pastor rose to begin the ceremony. Aunt Val's grip was still tight on my arm, and I wondered if the sadness of her mother's death was sinking in for her.

I, for once, didn't feel like a bomb ready to explode, though for some reason, I found myself wishing Kallias were there with me.

A door at the rear of the church slammed, causing everyone to jump. Dresses rustled, and I twisted with the rest of those present to see who the newcomer was.

My heart leapt. Kallias stood at the entrance to the church, dressed in black. Shirt and pants. The sight of him caused something warm and vulnerable to move through me.

But that was not what the rest of the congregation felt.

"Wolf!" Darion shouted.

Crossbows and other weapons were pulled from under benches and from underneath clothing, then pointed directly at Kallias. The warmth in my chest froze to terror.

"Wait!" I yelled, holding up my hands. "Don't shoot! I invited him."

A low murmur went through those present, and nobody moved.

"I invited him," I repeated. "Now put down your weapons."

Many lowered their weapons, though there was a lot of grumbling.

"What is in your head, girl? Inviting someone like that here, of all places?" Darion demanded.

I glanced at Aunt Val, who was silent, but the look on her face told me that the question was valid.

Kallias stood still, though he gazed around the room with caution. "Red's granny and I had a decent relationship. In honor of that, I decided to come and pay my respects."

"Well, I'm not staying with a wolf here," Darion snarled, and he lunged from the pew and marched for the side door.

My heart sank. Kallias remained at the other entrance, far from where Darion had been seated. What if he wasn't close enough to get a whiff of him? Then I'd endangered his life for nothing.

Warren must have seen the distress on my face and misinterpreted it because he squeezed my shoulder and said, "I'll speak with him." He moved out of the pew and pursued Darion out the side door.

Irvin stayed, his crossbow, along with a few weapons held by others who refused to lower them in the presence of a wolf, fixed on Kallias.

Kallias lifted his eyes to me, steel flickering in his gaze. "I am clearly not wanted here. So I will leave."

And with that, he turned to go, stepping out the church doors, letting them fall shut behind him. Relief slithered through me. He was out of the line of sight of the hunters' weapons. I wondered if he'd go after Darion to get his scent. I wanted to tell him to be careful.

But it was Granny's funeral.

I sat down next to Aunt Val.

"That man is your boyfriend?" Aunt Val's voice was tight but quiet.

I glanced at her for a moment, confused whether she meant Warren or Kallias. "Kallias . . ."

"Not the wolf," she hissed. "The man sitting with us. I know him. His real name is Roger Eckles. Years ago, when we were living on the outskirts of hunter territory, he came among us claiming his family had been slaughtered by wolves and that we needed to go to war against them. It got to where we had to expel him from our community."

I stared at Aunt Val, unsure of what to say. Warren? Good, safe, reliable Warren? "You must have him confused with someone else."

"I don't believe so. Be careful around him."

My head spun from Aunt Val's revelation. We had been together for almost a year, becoming serious shortly after he'd arrived. He'd always claimed his family lived in another town, but I never saw him write letters or try to contact them. Not once.

A scream pierced the air. My heart surged into my throat. Kallias— was he okay?

The whole gathering went still. It was clear the scream had come from outside the church. When another scream split the air, everyone burst into motion. I shoved Warren's jacket that he'd left in the pew aside as I reached for my crossbow. Some white pills fell from Warren's pocket, clinking against the floor.

Warning bells sounded in my mind, but I didn't have time to think about what they might mean. I scooped up a pill, grabbed my crossbow, and then leapt over the pews, shoving my way to the side door.

I burst outside. Somehow, Irvin, Darion's son, was right behind me.

I froze.

Darion lay in the grass not far from the church, his body mangled and ripped open. Dead.

Kallias, still in human form, crouched next to him. Not far away, a townswoman stood trembling. She must have been the person who had screamed.

Irvin whipped up his crossbow, and without consideration, I threw myself in front of him, blocking his view of Kallias.

"Move aside while I dispatch this murderous wolf," Irvin snarled at me.

"There is a rogue wolf." Kallias inched to his feet. "He killed Darion. If you let me go after him, I may still catch him."

"You expect me to believe that?" Irvin's hateful gaze snapped to meet Kallias's. "You're dead. You and all your kind. This is war."

"You are not the person to make that call, Irvin," I said. "I believe him. If you want to find your father's killer, he is the only one who can help."

"Then, with my father dead and no senior member to take his place, I put myself up for a vote as next order leader."

A fierceness shot through me. "And I will run against you."

Irvin looked ready to release his crossbow on me.

I held up my hands. "But now, let's catch a killer."

"Too many people will slow us down," Kallias said, glancing at the other attendees standing around. "I will take Red and Irvin only."

Irvin suddenly deflated. "This is not over, wolf." His gaze dropped to me; devastation mixed with his rage. "I must stay and tend to Father. Go with him and see vengeance is done."

"I promise." I turned and hurried after Kallias.

As we walked, tension pricked every bone in my body. The pills that had fallen out of Warren's jacket. They hadn't been Granny's blood pressure pills. I pulled one out of my pocket and my heart sank. I'd helped Lexa at her father's pharmacy enough to recognize it.

A sleeping pill.

I trembled. Warren had been picking up Granny's medicine. He must have found a way to sneak a few sleeping pills while he was at it. Maybe there was a reason I'd overslept the morning after Granny's murder. But my brain was having problems processing it.

I glanced at Kallias, who prowled a little ahead of me. "I might know who is working with the rogue wolf."

"Do you?"

I nodded, still not believing myself as I said it out loud. "Warren, my . . . boyfriend."

Kallias's brows drew together as we moved away from town and into the cover of the trees, leaving the funeral far behind. "There is something I should tell you. This rogue is most likely someone you know."

"What makes you say that?"

"Ever since our first meeting, I've smelled him on you."

I stopped in my tracks and stared at him. "What?"

"At first, I suspected you had had a run-in with our kind, maybe killed one of us. But then the next time we met, the scent was just as strong, and I thought . . ."

"What did you think?"

His jaw clenched, and he shook his head. "It doesn't matter. I smelled him again when I entered the church, but this time it was much stronger. Then, when Darion and that man sitting with you left, it grew fainter."

Dread curled in my stomach. "What are you saying?"

"Was that man sitting next to you, Warren?"

A clicking brought our gazes up to the trees. Warren stood with his crossbow in hand. He pulled the trigger, and the bolt sprung forward, burying its silver tip into Kallias's chest.

"I'm her boyfriend, dog," Warren snarled.

Horror bloomed in my heart as Kallias collapsed to the ground, blood pooling onto his shirt. I raised my eyes to Warren, who stared down on him, a look of pure satisfaction on his face.

My mind was muddled from what I was seeing. From what I was feeling. "No, Warren, you can't be the rogue. The wolves, they attacked your family—"

"And left me as one of them. They left me alive to spread the word of their ruthlessness. But would anyone listen? No. Not until I showed what a wolf can really do." His lip curled. "And now with his death at your hands and your death seeming to come from the pack as retribution, the war will start here, and I will see that it spreads until every wolf is wiped from this godforsaken country."

Brown fur sprouted from his skin, and his piercing blue eyes glowed. He dropped onto all fours, his body snapping and contorting. I raised my crossbow to shoot, but he lunged forward faster than I could respond, and with a swipe of his huge paw, he knocked it from my grasp. I swore and stumbled back as Warren stalked forward, teeth bared, ready to rip into my flesh. His gaze that had once held such concern and compassion now only held one thing. Hunger.

My body screamed at me to run, but there was no way I could outrun this agile beast. The pulsing beat of my heart in my ears would be the last thing I heard.

I was done for.

A howl sounded from behind, and a large black wolf lunged forward, attacking Warren. He was huge and majestic and had a silver-tipped bolt protruding from his chest.

Kallias.

The two wolves snarled and fought, but Kallias was injured and no match for Warren. The large brown wolf forced Kallias down, and I flinched at his loud yelp. A stone lodged in my throat.

Kallias.

The shock in my gut hardened into something cold and sure. I couldn't let Warren kill him. I ran and snatched up my crossbow.

Warren had killed Granny.

More wolves had arrived, ready to join the fight, but Warren bit into Kallias's throat and held him there, a snarl issuing up from him.

The other wolves sensed the warning. If they attacked, their leader would be killed.

Warren had tried to kill me. He'd tricked me. He wanted to start a war between the wolves and the hunters, destroying everything Granny had worked for.

I lifted my crossbow. Kallias had protected me. I wouldn't let him die trying to keep me safe. Taking aim, I let the silver-tipped bolt fly.

The bolt lodged in Warren's right eye.

He dropped Kallias, and fell to the earth, instantly dead.

I said I'd make Granny's killer pay. And I had.

The beautiful white wolf came forward and transformed into a woman. She knelt next to Kallias, examining him. I dropped the crossbow and hurried to her side. His fur appeared matted and wet. Crimson blood dripped into the dirt, and I beheld the bite marks where Warren's teeth had sunk into Kallias's throat.

"Is he going to be okay?" My voice shook.

She gazed at me with eyes that matched Kallias's and shook her head. "He's dying. But you can save him."

I looked at her, confused. "How can I save him?"

Her amber eyes flashed with meaning. "Only his mate can save him."

My mouth fell open. "His . . . What?"

"You can save him."

The universe was spinning out of control. "I . . . I'm not his mate."

"Why do you think he helped you? Why do you think we stood down when you ordered us to? Even your scent, he believed was wolfish because you were his mate."

My scent. Kallias must have thought my scent was that of a wolf because I was his mate. But that was a mistake. But the wolves *had* listened to me when I told them not to attack Lexa. Kallias had helped me, protected me for no reason.

Could it be true?

"How?" I asked.

"He must bite you. It will seal your mate-bond and then he can use your shared energy to help him heal. It is the only way."

"But won't I turn?" Turning into a wolf was against the contract between hunters and werewolves. Not to mention that mating with one was an act of war.

"Yes," the woman said.

Kallias's breaths came out sharp and wheezy, and an unexplained panic clenched my abdomen.

He couldn't die. I wanted to see him smile again. I wanted his warmth to rush over me.

Even if it broke the pact. Even if it meant becoming a wolf myself.

I wouldn't let him die.

But maybe, if I was discrete, I could hide it from the hunters and forestall war. I rolled up my sleeve and pressed my bicep near Kallias's snout. He jerked his head, letting out a low whine. And I understood. He refused to turn me.

"Please, Kallias. Don't make me live without you."

Kallias's deep eyes took me in. His tail thumped on the ground. His mouth opened, showing his sharp canines. He closed it around my arm, his warm tongue running gently over me before his teeth sank into my skin.

The End.

J. Ann Curtis

J. Ann Curtis is an award-winning author who has been making stories up in her head for as long as she can remember. Her YA Fantasy debut novel, *Lies of the Haven*, won best YA Fiction in the state of Nevada through the Indie Authors Project. When she is not writing, she is reading, and spending time with her husband and two amazing daughters.

To learn more about J. Ann Curtis and her writing, You can also check out her website at jacurtisbooks.com

2

Arachne

KATHERINE DICKERSON AND
ROSE KEMSLEY

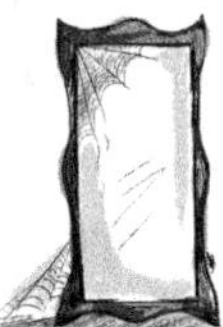

They were lost. Meredith shifted her map of the Appalachian, look-ing at it sideways, searching for the trail. But either the map was wrong or the trail wasn't on it.

Summer sun filtered through the branches to beat against her neck, threatening to turn her blanched skin red. Sweat dampened her arm-pits, and insects droned beside her face with an incessant *bzzzz.* Her three companions tugged on their shirts to fan themselves.

"Need help with that?" Theo asked, gesturing to the map.

"No. This trail isn't on here." If she couldn't find it, her husband wouldn't either. It was easier to figure it out herself.

She shoved the map back into her pocket and reached for Theo's hand, but he drew back—out of reach. Her hand swiped through empty air. She glanced at Theo, searching for any sign of frustration behind his umber eyes, any explanation for the rejected hand-hold. She saw none. He wasn't even looking at her. He smiled at their two friends, the expression crinkling the rich brown skin of his face, reminding her of the folds of crepe myrtle bark she sometimes peeled back in search of insects.

Had Theo noticed her attempted hand-hold? She'd sacrificed her time with her spiders to come here for him, and he had to appreciate that. Right? Maybe he wasn't trying to slight her, his attention was just elsewhere.

"We haven't passed any other hikers for like an hour." Craissada flipped her auburn braid over one shoulder.

"We'll figure it out." Theo smiled at Craissada, playing the role of the confident leader. But his optimism probably had less to do with confidence and more to do with the fact that he'd suggested this trip and he didn't want it to go wrong.

Groaning, Craissada threw her new pack to the ground, its price tag swaying with the impact. "Then I'm taking a break while you figure it out. It's hot as hell out here." She plopped down on a nearby stump. With her new hiking poles, her perfect mascara, and her overachieving profession, Craissada reminded Meredith of a trashline orbweaver. The orbweaver, a common, unremarkable spider, adorned its web with dried husks of insects, like decorations. It compensated for its shortcomings with each new addition, demanding notice.

"What? Too far for you?" Ben teased Craissada.

"I told you, I'm not much of a hiker. I haven't had time for this kind of stuff since starting residency, and my boots aren't broken in." Craissada massaged her ankles.

"I'm surprised you managed to come at all. I've barely seen you since we graduated. Do they shackle you to the hospital beds or something?" Ben smirked.

"If I'm going to graduate at the top of my residency class, I have to pretty much live at the hospital."

"Because it's not enough to already be a freaking *doctor,*" Ben drawled.

"Do you even want to be a doctor?" Meredith added.

In college, Meredith and Craissada shared a few science classes, but Craissada never seemed to enjoy them. She just plowed forward, relentless as a hurricane, stormy enough to scare everyone off.

"What do you mean? I've worked my ass off for this. I've had to." Craissada thrust a trekking pole into the ground with far too much gusto.

"We know, we know." Ben waved an exasperated hand. "You had to work twice as hard because you came from a bunch of crappy homes."

Meredith froze, prey sensing a predator, wishing she could scurry away like one of her jumping spiders. She sensed Theo stilling too. They all knew Craissada was raised in foster care, but they never talked about it. Or they hadn't in college. Maybe their dynamic had changed after five years apart. Maybe they shouldn't have tried to recreate the hiking trip from their senior year of college. Or maybe the heat was making them say things they shouldn't.

Craissada lifted her other pole, pointing its lethal tip at Ben. "You're an asshole. Maybe my job's competitive, but at least I've got one. What do you do again? A bunch of Instagram posts without your shirt?"

"As it turns out, people are willing to pay a lot of money to see me shirtless."

Meredith still didn't understand his job—*jobs*—which involved some mix of brand testing, car flipping, and gym selfies that showed off the abs under his perpetually spray-tanned skin, which had been as pale as hers in college. At some point, she'd stopped caring about his job. At some point, she'd stopped caring about him. Sure, in college, he'd kept Craissada from living in the library and Meredith from living in the lab. But in the five years since graduating, she'd only seen him a handful of times. Who was he to her now? Who was Craissada to her now?

"And has your perfect physique finally won you a girlfriend?" Craissada asked Ben. "One who wants to stick with you for more than a couple weeks?"

Ben opened his mouth, ready for a retort, but Theo stepped between them, a wide wall of muscle cutting off their argument. "There's a path over here. You think we should take it, Ben?" His voice pitched too high, tight with stress.

Ben glared at him, probably annoyed at the contrived interruption. There weren't any other paths around. They'd scoured the area already, and there definitely wasn't—

To Meredith's right, a narrow path appeared, shimmering into focus. She shifted, angling toward it.

At first, she thought Theo had spotted a game trail. But this trail was too trampled, an inelegant attempt at navigating around branches and tangles of plants. Goosebumps rose through the sunscreen slathered over her arms. That path hadn't been there before. She knew it hadn't.

A magnetic force drew her toward it, as if calling to her, and she took several steps closer. The trees there clumped densely, casting shadows despite the midday sun. The shadows shifted and swayed, as if alive, or as if something inside them was. A chilly breeze wafted over Meredith, offering welcome relief, and she found her feet carrying her toward the path of their own accord.

"We don't know where this leads. Or if it's safe. It's too risky to go off-trail in the Appalachians," Meredith argued, though she continued toward the path.

"We went off trail last time, and it was amazing," Ben countered.

"That was five years ago. We were young and dumb." Even back then she'd thought going off trail was stupid. Despite her doubts, though, her traitorous feet kept taking her closer.

"We're lost, anyway. And this path has some shade. Don't tell me the *ecologist* is scared of exploring some leaves and twigs," Ben quipped, bounding ahead of her to slip between the Virginia creepers and ferns.

Meredith pursed her lips. The *ecologist.* Because that's what she was now. The ecologist, not Meredith.

"The ecologist is too busy studying her lab spiders to run around outside with wild ones," Theo teased.

"That research has earned me two publications in *Ecological Entomology,*" Meredith defended herself. She realized too late she didn't need to name the journal. It didn't matter how prestigious it was within ecological circles, none of them would've heard of it.

"I guess the publications make up for not hiking then. My wife's a genius, everybody." Theo winked at her.

Meredith couldn't tell if he was complimenting her or complaining because she didn't do more outdoorsy stuff with him. His job was never as demanding as hers, so he didn't understand being strapped for time like she did.

Theo gave her a winning grin, tilting his head while squinting against the sun. She remembered a younger Theo striking that exact pose five years ago, sunlight reflecting off his skin, thumbs looped into the straps of the same hiking pack on the Appalachian Trail. Back then, they'd just gotten engaged, and he reminded her of *Platycryptus undatus*: a tan and brown jumping spider with a personality as playful as its name. The arachnids matched Theo's skin tone and often enjoyed crawling into people's hands to explore. Theo had personified that brave adventurer.

Now, Theo better resembled a yellow sac spider, an aggressive house pest fated to bite unprovoked. Sometimes, Meredith couldn't tell whether she'd been bitten. Theo would sleep on the couch instead of in bed with her, then text her in the morning and tell her to *have a great day at work*. He'd "forget" about their dinner reservation, but still fold her laundry the next day.

Maybe, he'd never bitten her, and she'd just imagined the inconsistency in their relationship. Or maybe she had his venom in her veins, and he was off spinning a sac to hide inside.

When Craissada, then Theo stepped onto the path, Meredith hesitated. But she was outvoted, both by her companions and her own feet, so she followed, taking up the rear.

The moment her foot touched the dirt-worn path, the woods tilted. The earth shifted under her feet, and she yelped, leaning against a nearby trunk for balance. The light overhead blinked in and out for a few moments like a sketchy Motel Six, then it coughed in a last attempt at brilliance before pitching them into darkness. The heat vanished along with the sun, and a damp chill settled through the woods. Birds stopped mid-song, strangled on dying notes, and the lulling buzz of insects whispered into the silence. The breeze vanished, leaving only the blackened sky to stretch grappling fingers through the branches.

Meredith searched the blackness for her friends, but she couldn't see them. "What happened? Something's wrong—" Meredith cut off halfway through the word, the rest of the letters slipping from her tongue like rain off a frog. Her mouth hung open, waiting for the right syllables to fall out of it as she fought to remember what she was about to say. It was important, whatever it was. Or . . . was it? With each elongated second, her forgotten phrase felt less and less relevant. The dark, now invading the woods, penetrated her mind, obscuring her thoughts in a hazed twilight. When she contemplated her worry, it dissipated around her like fog between her fingers.

She grappled through the dark until she found Theo beside her, and she let out a breath, relieved her companions remained with her. Theo swung off his pack to find a flashlight. Ahead of her, lights blinked into focus as Craissada and Ben switched on lanterns, which cast lighted circles just bright enough to walk by. The trees crowded closer as if watching them. Their trunks and leaves had turned gray, like the dried husks of bugs in a web. The only vibrancy came from the crimson fungi crawling up their trunks. The fungi oozed against the bark, half-liquid, and trickles of red dribbled down like blood.

"We need to find somewhere to camp," Theo announced, uncertainty breathing between each word.

"Somewhere with enough space for all of us. I need at least fifteen feet between my tent and Sir Snores-a-Lot," Ben said, pointing at Theo. He spoke too loud, forcing an unnatural level of pep into his voice.

"I don't snore!"

Ben guffawed. "You snore twice as loud as you talk, which is saying something. Be glad you've still got a wife"

"Says the guy who's never stayed with the same woman for more than a month," Theo teased back.

Ben shrugged, his muscled shoulders straining against his far-too-tight shirt. "It would be a crime to reserve this for only one woman. Sharing is caring." He flexed his arms, winking at Theo.

Meredith blinked, glancing between them. How could they be talking about snoring right now? How come no one else seemed concerned? Were they just pretending not to be? A primal part of Meredith screamed at her to run, hide, anything to get away from the wrongness.

But the fog that had invaded her mind blanketed her concerns, smothering them. It lulled her senses and fragmented her memory, making it impossible to remember how the forest had looked earlier. What color had the leaves been? No. They must've always been gray. Her friends were acting normal, so she needed to act normal too.

She didn't know how long they walked. No stars lit their way, and only the bobbing of lanterns and flashlights gave any indication of forward motion. Occasionally, an unfamiliar scent wafted past, sweet and poignant enough to make her gag. It reminded her of burnt sugar, though she couldn't identify it, just like she couldn't name the pervasive fungus.

When Theo's lantern revealed a tent ahead, they quickened their pace to investigate. A pair of hiking sandals rested beside the open structure, along with a folded set of cargo pants, a pink and black polka-dotted sweatshirt, and a Camelbak. Inside lay an unrolled sleeping bag and pillow, both without a single crease, as if on display for Eastern Mountain Sports.

They stared. Craissada lifted her lantern higher, accentuating the pockmarks of acne scarring her tawny cheeks. She narrowed her eyes and ran a hand over her braid, lips puckering into a frown, though she said nothing.

"Where's the camper?" Meredith whispered.

"Probably off enjoying the stars somewhere," Craissada ventured.

"Probably off enjoying *someone* somewhere," Ben smirked.

Meredith glanced toward the woods, the yawning black that felt more suitable for a tomb than a liaison, then at the sky, where not a single star gleamed from between the heavy branches. Something was strange about this, but she couldn't figure out what. She felt as if she were underwater, swimming with her eyes open, squinting to make out something that should be obvious.

"I'm sure they're fine. I bet the next clearing will be big enough for all our tents," Theo offered, grinning.

Did he not sense anything odd about a hiker venturing into the woods without their shoes or clothes in the middle of the night? Or did he just feel like he had to keep them going since he'd organized this hiking reunion trip? He continued on the path, and one by one, they each followed.

After a stretch, they came to another tent. Again, an open flap revealed an untouched sleeping mat with perfectly folded blankets atop it. A pair of pants, a black shirt with a picture of mountains, a hydro flask, and a rain poncho sat in a neat line amid the moss, untouched.

They ventured deeper into the wood, their lanterns' pathetic pin-pricks of light fending off a vast and impenetrable darkness. At the third campsite, they found a pair of sleeping bags, a folded pile of men's clothes, a pile of women's clothes, and a set of matching hiking poles. At the fourth, they found five tents, their openings all facing away from each other, each with its own set of organized hiking essentials, as if they'd stumbled on some progressive museum of hiking rather than an actual trail.

"They're fine," her companions murmured. "Everyone's fine." Their expressions wavered between panic and confidence, as confused as Meredith's own reactions were. Why would *all* of these hikers leave their tents in the middle of the night?

Meredith considered saying that this didn't feel fine at all. But as soon as she opened her mouth, she forgot what she was going to say. A soothing sense of oblivion blurred her worry, like the forgetfulness from when she'd had one too many cranberry vodkas in college. Her friends weren't freaking out. She was just overreacting.

When they reached a clearing wide enough for them all, Craissada threw off her new pack and groaned. They set up camp in silence, casting glances at each other, daring each other to speak. No one did. Meredith sidestepped crimson puddles from the fungi as she and Theo passed poles and stakes between them. They retreated into their respective tents and into themselves, hiding from each other behind walls of nylon.

When Meredith tried to kiss her husband goodnight, he shifted away. He fiddled with his shoelaces without meeting her eyes, then crawled into his sleeping bag in silence.

Something like anger flowed through the confusion, clouding Meredith's thoughts. Did he not want to kiss her? Was he trying to manipulate her into feeling . . . what? Guilty? She hadn't wanted to go camping with Ben and Craissada, who she'd barely spoken to for five years. Theo was the one who'd wanted to recreate their epic camping adventure from their senior year of college. She would've preferred to stay in her lab with her jumping spiders.

But Theo had seemed so upset after losing his job. He said he was fine, but he'd started avoiding her, spinning a web to crawl inside and hide, just like a damned yellow sac spider. Without meaning to, she'd started avoiding him too, staying later and later at work. When he'd suggested camping, she hadn't felt like refusing was an option. If he was willing to climb out of that sac, she needed to encourage it.

Or so she'd thought. A heavy sense of rejection pressed her into her sleeping bag. For half a moment, she wondered if they should talk to a marriage counselor.

Meredith rejected the thought. Telling someone about their relationship could complicate it more, especially if she'd been misinterpreting his actions. It was easier to just figure it out on her own. Anyway, if Theo were upset about something, he'd tell her. Right?

Meredith listened for anything other than the silence enveloping them. She considered asking Theo if he'd noticed the unnatural quiet, but talking about it could make it real. If anything got stranger, she'd deal with it herself.

Meredith never found rest that night. She fought through half-conjured dreams where she couldn't distinguish where consciousness ended and the subconscious began. She pictured herself in her lab, examining her jumping spiders. The arachnids climbed up through the open lid of their enclosure to scurry over her hands. They tip-toed up her arms, tickling her with their pedipalps, then scaled her neck and jaw to whisper into her ears, *"What are you doing here? With them? You belong back in the lab, where you thrive. Come and find us, Meredith."* They scurried from her ears onto her face, their tiny feet tapping rhythms against her cheeks as they neared her mouth, the fine hairs along their tarsi brushing over her parted lips as they climbed inside—

Meredith bolted upright, wiping her mouth as if to ward off her spiders. She reached for her husband's hand, but her fingers grazed against an empty sleeping bag. "Theo?"

Silence replied.

"Theo, where are you?"

Sweat slicked along her back as she fumbled through the tent to find her flashlight. A horizontal pillar of light rolled over the sleeping bags, illuminating an empty tent. Theo's sleeping bag appeared neatly made as if he'd never slept there at all.

Her heart throbbed in her throat. Blonde locks fell into her face as she staggered out of the tent and yanked on her boots. Theo's only pair of shoes sat outside in the dirt.

Fear filtered through the blanket of oblivion obscuring her thoughts. Where could he have gone without his shoes? About ten feet away, a pile of clothes and shoes sat in a neat pile by Ben's tent. Meredith jogged over and threw open the tent flap, but Ben wasn't inside. Craissada's tent had the same perfect pile of hiking supplies, minus the hiker.

Meredith whirled, taking in the abandoned campsite, suddenly dizzy.

Meredith. Find me.

Theo's pained voice echoed from beyond the clearing, farther down the off-trail, disjointed and gargled.

"Theo?" Meredith rushed toward his voice, flashlight revealing the bouncing flashes of twisted, gnarled branches that reached toward her like the spindly legs of a cellar spider. She sprinted through a twisting course between the trees, not sure whether she was even following the trail.

Meredith. Find me. Panic shrieked through his plea.

With each stride, her mind pinpointed a single thought: find Theo.

As she ran, light filtered through the woods. A gray, dull glow alleviated the blackness, transforming it from night into something like a colorless sunrise. Tepid, uncertain rays snuck between the bushes, reflecting off the crimson fungus. With the new light, Meredith could make out the woods thinning ahead. The underbrush grew sparser, and beyond it, she saw . . . asphalt? A house? She pushed through the remaining distance, and burst across the tree line into—

A cul-de-sac.

A suburban neighborhood stretched in front of her with a series of bland, two-story houses painted in grays. She panted at the rounded end of the cul-de-sac, the kind kids used for bikes and scooters. Not that any bikes or scooters littered the sidewalks. Or a single person. Every house had their blinds drawn and their lights out, and no cars parked in the driveways. It looked like a model of suburbia, a museum of the American middle class, just like the *museum of hiking* she'd passed in the woods.

Something about this situation didn't make sense. This neighborhood shouldn't be here, but she couldn't recall why. Her boots scuffed against the cement as she jogged down the sidewalk. "Theo?"

Meredith. Hear me.

His voice floated from the first house on the street, a pristine white facade with an immaculate yard of cut grass. She barreled through the unlocked front door, sure she'd find Theo inside.

But she found no one.

A set of stairs extended in front of the entryway. To her left, the home opened into a dining room with an oval table large enough to seat a family. Though no family sat there. It looked as if no one had ever sat there. Empty picture frames hung on the walls. Generic furniture decorated the space, factory-issued chairs and lamps that screamed "model home." To her right, a full-length mirror hung on the wall, reflecting the dining room. But not reflecting her.

Meredith took a step closer to the mirror and pressed her fingers against its chill surface. She couldn't remember—was she supposed to be able to see herself in it?

Shaking her head, she lowered her hand. If Theo wasn't down here, maybe he was upstairs. She bounded up the steps two at a time and ventured onto the second level.

But the moment she stepped onto the landing, she found herself back at the bottom of the stairs. Meredith blinked, eyebrows knitting together as her legs tensed, ready to run, though she didn't know what she needed to run from. She swiveled, checking that she was back where she'd started: the same blank mirror, the same family dining table without the family. She'd gone up the stairs, hadn't she?

Again, she bounded up the steps. Again, she found herself back at the bottom. This time though, she noticed something—someone—in the mirror to her right. Meredith stumbled back, swallowing a scream.

A woman without a mouth stood inside the mirror. Smooth skin stretched under her nose to a lipless chin. Wide, terrified eyes met Meredith's as the woman hugged herself, rocking back on her heels.

Meredith whirled, searching the room for the woman, but she was alone. The glass no longer reflected the dining room. It only displayed the woman, as if she stood a few feet in front of her, separated by a window, trapped.

Panic sliced through Merideth, overpowering the voice trying to convince her not to worry. She shoved off the blanket of oblivion, leaving herself chilled. This was not normal. A tremor coursed through her, and she tucked her elbows against her sides, making herself smaller.

Where the hell was this woman's mouth? No—how had she wound up in the mirror? She wore the same polka-dotted sweatshirt Meredith had seen while hiking, the one from the first vanished hiker. Tears rolled down the woman's cheeks and over the space where her mouth should've been, and Meredith didn't know whether to pity or fear her. "What happened to you? Can you get out?" Meredith asked.

The woman in the mirror shook her head. She dragged a fingernail along the mirror from the inside, and a grating *eeeee* shrieked through the entryway. Her nail scratched out one letter at a time, spelling UNWORTHY. The woman pointed to the word, then to herself.

What did that mean? The woman was unworthy of leaving the mirror? Meredith's breathing devolved into short, heaving gasps.

Meredith. Hear me.

Theo's desperate voice drifted through the front door, coming from farther down the street. With her eyes still fixed on the woman in the mirror, Meredith backed away.

Meredith. Hear me.

Heart throbbing against her ribcage, she bolted out the door. She raced down the sidewalk and into the next house, which had precisely the same layout as the first. The same oval table filled the dining room, and the same full-length mirror hung on the wall to her right. No one stood inside the house, though a man stood inside the mirror. He wore a black shirt with mountains on it, identical to the one she'd passed hiking. Like the woman, he had no mouth, just skin where his lips should've been. His fingernails screeched against the glass as he scratched out the word INCOMPETENT.

The man's brows fell in an expression of resignation as he stared at Meredith. She didn't stare back. She searched the dining room for Theo. After the staircase landed her by the front door for a third time and she still hadn't found him, she ran back out onto the sidewalk.

What if she couldn't find him? What if someone—some *thing*—was hurting him? She imagined Theo without a mouth, caught inside a spider's web, his brown skin paling as an unseen monster drained him of life.

She followed her husband's voice down the street, stopping at each house. At each stop, she found the same mirror with a different mouthless person. They each scratched out a word for Meredith to read:

STUPID.

UNLOVABLE.

UGLY.

She fisted the fabric of her shirt, clutching at her chest as she panted. Still, she ran. She searched for any streets leading away, connecting to civilization. She found none. The neighborhood had a rounded cul-de-sac on both ends, shaping the whole thing like a massive bone, or an infinity sign in a never-ending suburban nightmare. Though the first houses on the street looked new, later houses became more decrepit, like a succession of old exoskeletons discarded by a molting spider. Tired paint peeled off in thin strips. Scuffs streaked across the front doors. Weeds invaded the front walk. By the tenth house, scratches marred the table and mirror inside, and stains decorated the carpeted stairs.

In that tenth house, Meredith finally met a familiar face in the mirror.

Ben's wide, blue eyes stared at her through the film of glass.

Meredith pressed her fists to the sides of her head, her shoulders hunching as she slouched. She dug her knuckles into her skull until it hurt.

Ben wore the same Adidas hiking sandals and striped T-shirt she'd found by his tent. But if Ben's clothes were at the campsite, how could they be here too? Maybe Ben wasn't a part of her world anymore.

Maybe Ben was dead.

As soon as she thought it, her mind electrified, embracing the idea, as if it had been waiting for her to make the realization. He was dead.

Dead. Dead. Dead.

Her whole body shook, and hair fell into her face, blocking her view of her once-friend. If Ben was dead, was Theo dead too? A strangled sound escaped her, fear overpowering any sense of sorrow. "What happened?"

Ben scratched out the word LONELY. He pointed to the word, then to himself.

Was he trying to say his loneliness had trapped him here? Could she get him out? She tried to pry the mirror from the wall, but when her hands touched it, an electric shock zapped through her. She gripped the frame as images of Ben flicked through her mind: Ben standing in his empty studio apartment, practicing his winning smile in his toaster's reflection. Ben asking if the woman getting dressed by his bed wanted to get brunch, only for her to wink at him and walk out. Ben staring at a text string with Craissada where she said, *too busy to talk rn.*

Meredith released the frame, panting as the images vanished. A stinging behind her nose and eyes warned her that tears were inevitable, though she tried to blink them back. Maybe she should've considered that Ben might be lonely since he didn't have a significant other and his job was always changing. But he'd never said anything. Or maybe she'd never really listened. If she had listened, if she'd cared enough to notice his loneliness, would it have made any difference for him?

Meredith. Understand me. Theo's voice whispered through a broken window in the dining room.

"Ben, where's Theo?" she demanded.

Ben only furrowed his brow.

"Where's Theo?" she screamed again, though he still didn't respond. She glanced between Ben and the window. She wanted to help him, but she didn't know how, and she had to find Theo to make sure he wasn't trapped too. "I'm so sorry," she murmured, not meeting his eyes as she sprinted toward the next house.

She didn't find Theo in the next house. Craissada sat on her knees inside the mirror, tears streaming down her mouthless face as she stared up at Meredith. Her nails screeched out the word INADEQUATE on the glass.

Meredith reached out, wondering if she'd feel the same electricity she had with Ben. As her fingertips met the glass, images of Craissada flashed before her: Craissada as a young girl, leaving a foster home with only a trash bag of clothes. Craissada on a park bench at night, finishing AP Calculus homework by cell phone light. Craissada reading the residency match list, searching for her name among the peers and colleagues who hadn't worked half as hard as she had.

Meredith had never thought of Craissada, the valedictorian in college and medical school, as INADEQUATE. Given her background, she understood why Craissada might think that about herself, but Meredith had never asked her about it. If she had, would it have made any difference?

It didn't matter right now. She had to find Theo. Meredith whispered an apology to Craissada, her voice breaking between short, terrified breaths as she pulled her hand away from the glass. She staggered out of the house and onto the sidewalk, heading toward the final house on the street. No paint remained on this sad excuse for a building, and the roof pitched inward in several spots. Floorboards creaked as she stepped into the entryway. She paused, collecting herself before entering, afraid of what she would find. Meredith inhaled, exhaled, then turned to her right.

Theo stared back at her from behind cracked glass.

Meredith fell to her knees. A sob bubbled up through her throat, but it stayed caught inside her, blocking her airway and making it impossible to breathe. When she opened her mouth to scream, nothing came out. Tears blurred the scuffed, warped floorboards as she hung her head. With her hands pressed into the rough floor, she looked up at her husband. Her eyes briefly met his before he drooped with regret.

She reached toward the mirror, and electricity sparked down her arm. Images of Theo ripped through her mind: Theo as a child waiting in the dark for his parents to pick him up after they'd forgotten about him. Theo's boss staring at his computer screen, not bothering to look at Theo as he tells him they're cutting his department. Theo sitting at their table set for two and eating alone while staring at an unanswered text to Meredith that asks when she'd get home from work.

She pounded her hands against the mirror in frustration, palms slicing on the cracked glass. Blood slipped over her wrist, stark crimson against her fair skin, dribbling like the seeping fungus on the trail. She drove her fingers into the cracks, desperate to yank out the shards and get her husband out. But the cracks remained immovable, and she only succeeded in slicing her fingertips.

Theo watched her efforts with slumped shoulders, chin lowered. Her blood smeared over his facade, seeping into each cracked crevice until his visage ran red. "I'm getting you out," she told him, tears trailing down her face.

Theo just shook his head, as if to say, "No. You're not." He scratched the word INSIGNIFICANT into the glass.

But Theo wasn't insignificant. Not to her.

Maybe she hadn't done a great job of showing him that. Her work had always been demanding. Even before Theo lost his job, she'd made more money than him, so she'd handled the financials in their marriage. They'd moved for her job instead of his, which made sense since she was more successful. It wasn't Theo's fault that she liked doing things her way. Even in her marriage, she insisted on doing things alone.

Meredith pounded on the mirror again. When she tried to yank her hand back though, it stuck to the glass, like a fly stuck in a web. Her fingers slipped through it as if something were tugging her into the mirror with him, silken fibers reeling her in. The sob caught in her throat shuddered, then vanished. Her breathing slowed. A heavy sense of release coursed through her limbs like venom, paralyzing her. The mirror dulled her pain, dulled everything, and drew her closer. She leaned farther into the glass, until her entire forearm slipped through it, and the sense of relief strengthened.

Theo's face faded from the mirror, and instead, a cluster of scarlet spiders appeared behind the glass. Hundreds of them hung from glistening ruby fibers, suspended in midair, though she couldn't tell what they were suspended from. They looked nothing like any arachnid she knew or had studied. They twisted and swung, delicate legs wheeling through the air as they spun a web that looked remarkably like letters. She recognized a P first, then an R, and after an efficient flurry of legs and spinnerets, the arachnids finished the word PRIDE.

Her sense of relief faltered. Was that word meant for her? Guilt battled against the relief flowing from the mirror. Sure, Meredith struggled with pride. But it's not like she went around telling everyone she was better than them. She just liked to get things done herself.

She could allow the mirror to consume her and take her pride with it. Maybe she could be with Theo on the other side. At the thought of Theo, the image of him replaced the spiders in the mirror. Her gaze met his, expecting him to welcome her, but only fear crept through his umber eyes.

She hesitated. Had Theo, Craissada, Ben, and all the others intentionally tangled themselves in the web? Let the mirror swallow them? Is that how they'd . . . died?

It would be easier to fall through the glass, to let it devour her pain and pride and leave her empty. But is that what she wanted? Easy and empty?

She'd never directly confronted Theo about what was wrong because that would have been admitting something was wrong. It was easier not to go to therapy, just like it was easier to read the map by herself and financially support their marriage by herself. Help was only a synonym for hurt.

She'd thought she was independently dealing with her issues. But what if she'd really just been avoiding them? It was all any of them had done. None of them had been willing to confront their pain or talk about it. This place fed on their unspoken torments, devouring them, growing with each new person in the mirrors. The perfect predator.

She strained, yanking her arm back, but the mirror only seemed more determined to drag her in.

Theo's chest rose and fell with heavy breaths. He pointed toward her, then the door, gesturing for her to run.

She fought against the mirror, pulling against the invisible silk wrapping around her forearm. Fibers snapped with tiny *plinks.* This thing, this monster, reached for more, no end to its appetite. She threw her weight into tearing away, until finally, she freed herself.

She kept her eyes trained on Theo's as she fumbled out the door and into the street. She didn't want to abandon him, but she didn't think she could do anything for him now. If she stayed, she'd wind up in a mirror too. "I'm sorry, Theo. I'm sorry . . . I'm . . . sorry . . . I'm . . ." Her panting drowned out her apology as she bolted down the street, searching for some way out of the neighborhood and the mirrored monster. Could she get out the way she'd come in? She ran the full length of the street, but saw nothing leading anywhere.

Meredith. Understand us. Theo, Craissada, and Ben's voices played through her head, the chorus of their unified voices drowning out any rational thought.

Meredith skidded to a stop and drove her hands into her hair, hunching, her forearms blocking her face. She needed out, out, out—

"Help!" Meredith dropped her hands, not sure who she was shouting to. "Please! I can't get out on my own." The last words came out as a whimper as she hugged herself, rocking slightly.

A path appeared.

Just wide enough for one person, an overgrown trail materialized between two houses with thousands, maybe millions, of the scarlet spiders scurrying over roots and rocks. It looked nothing like the path she'd entered from, and could be dangerous. But staying here, in the monster's web, was definitely dangerous.

Meredith. Understand us.

Meredith sprinted onto the path, stumbling over old root systems and oozing fungi. Spiders fell into her hair to scurry down her neck and beneath her shirt. Shrieking, she threw off her shirt, leaving only her sports bra on. Pinpricks of pain started on her arms, then spread to her shoulders as the arachnids began biting her.

She knocked spiders from body as she ran, not sure if these creatures wanted to poison or devour her. Behind her, the neighborhood had vanished. No rooftops rose among the trees, and no asphalt peeked between the branches. Instead, graying bodies hung from the canopy, suspended by amaranthine webs. A hollowed husk of what must've once been Craissada rotated above her, its pockmarked cheeks collapsed against its jaw. Ben's corpse hung beside it, its gray skin drained of its spray tan. Even Theo's corpse had turned pale, its eyes vacant as they stared into nothing, its mouth opened in a silent scream.

Or maybe not silent. Someone was screeching. No. She was screeching. Her raw throat and overtaxed lungs begged her to stop, but the sound only pitched higher.

PRIDE, the spiders wrote in the branches. The word hung between twigs, trunks, and trees, over the trail, enveloping the forest. Meredith pushed through webs, destroying dotted i's and curling p's, but the arachnids worked faster than she did. They built a wall of web across the path in overlapping letters, trapping her in, and Meredith drove her fingernails into her palms, drawing blood.

Bracing herself, she hurled herself at the wall. Web clung to her, and her muscles quivered as she pitched forward . . .

And landed on her side in the middle of a wide, sunny hiking trail.

Brilliant light shone above her, twinkling through the leaves with welcoming warmth. The spiders and corpses vanished, replaced with squirrels and chipmunks. The fog invading her mind dissipated. Birdsong trilled through the branches, along with the low hum of insects and the chatter of hikers. Everything smelled of scorched earth and summer blooms.

Meredith remained on her side, dirt smearing her ribs and falling into her sports bra. Ben. Craissada. Theo. Dead. Dead. Dead. Tears mixed with dirt to flow into her mouth, tasting of fear. When she tried to sit up, her muscles betrayed her, spasming and convulsing to make her flail. Rocks sliced into her convulsing limbs, though she barely registered her pain next to her grief.

A set of boots approached. She tried to readjust and see the people attached to those boots, but the forest spun and tilted around her, and she pressed her eyes shut. Meredith had always compared herself to her favorite spider, the *Phiddipus audax,* strong and unafraid, willing to take on prey twice its size. But now?

She was nothing. Nothing but a failed wife and failed friend with too much damn pride to realize how she'd hurt them.

"What happened?" A concerned feminine voice asked.

She opened her eyes, fixing her tilting gaze on a pair of bright pink boots.

A monster killed my friends, and only I survived. But she didn't know how to tell her that.

"Are you all right?" the woman asked.

"No," Meredith gasped. She exhaled, lifting a trembling finger to her mouth, smearing blood over her lips. "I need help." Her eyes met the woman's, and a spot of movement near the woman's collar caught her attention. She stilled as a scarlet spider crawled out from under the woman's shirt to travel up her neck and disappear into her hair.

Rose Kemsley

Rose grew up with eight siblings, each with a love of reading, and a love of spoiling endings for anyone who didn't read them fast enough. After a childhood of raiding her sisters' libraries and hiding with books under the gym bleachers, she pursued her love of literature with an English degree at Brigham Young University. Now a mother of two girls and an award-winning writer, she still hides with her books in closets, though at least now she can call it a career choice instead of being antisocial.

Katherine Dickerson

Katherine spent most of her childhood either watching nature documentaries or exploring the outdoors. That childhood pastime morphed into a deep appreciation for the environment, especially the world of insects and spiders. She received her Master of Science from the University of Nebraska Kearney and now works to promote environmental stewardship. She has since passed this respect for Mother Nature onto her three sons, who are learning to appreciate the environment and the world of creepy crawlers just as much as their mom.

3

I'm Innocent

LAURA M. DRAKE

The phone's shrill tone sounded through the Bluetooth speaker into my ear. I drummed my fingers on the steering wheel's supple leather as the call went to voicemail. Again.

"Hey, Mom, I'm on my way with dinner. Call me back."

It wasn't like her not to answer, but she was probably napping. She'd been doing that more and more lately as the cancer got worse. I'd told her multiple times she should live with me, something we'd done for a few years after her divorce while I finished school. Despite my pleas, she insisted on living alone, saying she didn't want to cramp my style, and she'd only grown more adamant once I'd started dating Denzel. We both knew it was a miracle I'd developed feelings for someone after everything that had happened in the past.

Today's paperwork had taken longer than expected—it always did—and I was later than what Mom expected. Last night, I'd said seven.

It was almost eight, and the scent of soy and ginger wafting from the takeout containers in the passenger seat made my stomach grumble.

I'd gotten sushi to celebrate wrapping up another murder investigation—my usual ritual with Mom, ever since becoming a detective. She'd always been invested in my work, asking questions about how we caught our suspects, and mourning the unsolved cases with me. Lately, she'd been even more curious, as if trying to cram all the questions she wouldn't be able to ask later into our last few months together.

Ten minutes after leaving work, I turned into her subdivision and passed the well-manicured lawns of her neighbors, who had *way too much time on their hands*, as Mom always said. I always laughed at that since Mom spent pretty much all of her retirement either with her crochet hook or her book club. I parked in the driveway and opened the car door.

"Slow down, Evelyn!" Mr. Warner poked his head up above his overly-symmetrical hedges. "You're going to kill someone, driving like that!"

No one got away with anything with Mr. Warner around. He seemed to have nothing better to do than spy on the neighbors.

"Sorry," I called back as I retrieved the sushi from the passenger seat and closed the door with my foot. It slammed shut with a bang that echoed throughout the quiet neighborhood like a gunshot.

"First that nutcase in the black car, now you," he muttered in a voice that carried over the picket fence Mom had painted pink on her side just to spite him. "I need to have a talk with your mother about her visitors . . ."

I ignored him and walked up the front steps, inhaling the scent of hydrangeas and pine. After passing under the arch of the front porch, I scrounged in my bag for Mom's house key, but came up short. I must've left it at home. Instead, I rang the doorbell, then stepped back and studied the peeling gray paint, which could use another coat. A brisk fall wind cut through my jacket, and I shivered.

Where was Mom? I twisted the top of the sushi bag around my fingers, winding it and unwinding it. After a few moments, I leaned closer to the door and made out hushed voices. Was someone with her? That wasn't too unusual, but she didn't mention anyone joining us.

I looked down at my hand. I'd wrapped the plastic so tight, I'd cut off circulation.

"Come on, Mom," I muttered as I knocked and loosened the bag.

The door creaked open at my touch, and the hairs on the back of my neck rose.

Something was wrong. Even last summer when her air conditioner had broken, Mom refused to leave her door open.

My body tingled in tense anticipation. I carefully put the bag of food down and slipped inside, ignoring the meticulously arranged shoes at the entrance and the smell of potpourri that assaulted my nose.

An unnatural stillness hung in the air, making my pulse race. My fingers twitched for the gun I didn't wear off duty.

I crept down the hall to the living room and found the television playing an Andy Griffith re-run in an empty room. That explained the voices, but where was—

A pair of familiar pink slippers stuck out from the other side of the faded plaid couch.

"Mom!" The ragged cry tore from my throat. I rushed to her side and dropped to my knees, pressing two fingers to her neck. The rapid thud of my heartbeat only emphasized the lack of hers. The sightless way her empty gaze stared at the ceiling. She wore the nightgown I'd given her five years ago, though I'd told myself this was the year I'd finally buy her a new one. The soft throw from the couch partially shrouded her body, as if she'd grabbed it while falling.

"Please, please, please," I muttered, although her stiff body, cool skin, and motionless chest told me everything I needed to know. Mom had been gone for hours.

I fumbled for my phone and made a call with shaking fingers.

"Nine-one-one. What's the location of your emergency?" a cool voice on the other end of the line answered.

"My mom. She's . . ." I choked back tears as an icy sensation spread through my chest. I wrapped my hand around my necklace, letting the smooth metal ground me.

"Ma'am, what is your location?"

My training kicked in and the panic and grief curled up in a corner of my mind. Methodically, I answered her questions.

After hanging up, I held Mom's hand—a final moment for just the two of us. "I love you to the moon and back, Mom," I whispered, repeating the line she'd told me every night as she tucked me in as a child.

I drew in a shuddering breath, stood, and called Denzel.

"Couldn't wait to talk to me again, eh?" His deep voice came through the phone over the background noise of the station. His steady, reassuring cadence released my carefully locked-up emotions. "Aren't you supposed to be with your mother for dinner?"

Emotion clogged my throat. I couldn't say the words a second time.

A beat of quiet came from the other end, highlighting the racket from the television. My silence told him everything I couldn't. "I'm so sorry, Ev. I'm on my way."

"Thanks."

"I know you weren't expecting her to go so soon, but the cancer was spreading—"

"No, that can't be it. It just doesn't feel right." Tears burned at my eyes, but I inhaled sharply and blinked them away. "She had months to live. Nothing about this feels right."

The sound of Denzel's car door opening and closing came through the speaker, then he said, "I don't think losing a parent is supposed to feel right."

"We should still have time together." My shoes squeaked on Mom's overly-clean linoleum as I moved into the kitchen.

Another long moment where I could imagine the way Denzel would look at me with sympathy filling his dark eyes. "Ev—"

"Don't *Ev* me," I snapped at him, letting my frustration sweep away the numbing grief. "Her door was open when I got here. Don't you think that's weird?" I traced a trembling finger over Mom's collection of crocheted pot holders that hung from hooks on the wall. *How could it have been just last Saturday that we were in here baking cookies together?*

"Maybe she forgot to shut it when she came home. Or maybe the door didn't latch correctly." Despite my anger, his tone was soft and careful. "Sometimes people just die, Ev. You can't treat everything like a case."

Maybe I was grasping at straws. Just because her door was open didn't make this a crime scene. I looked away from the wall, my gaze snagging on two mugs resting in the sink. The only hint of her presence in the otherwise spotless kitchen. "Someone was here today."

"Why do you say that?"

"Because there's another cup in the sink. And Mom always does the dishes before bed." I stared at the cups, one from our trip to Disneyland and another that said *World's Best Mom.*

"It was probably just someone from her book club or something."

"Maybe." I turned down the hall, racking my brain for anything Mom had said about having company today. The pale-blue carpet muffled the sound of my footsteps in the hall. If only it could muffle the pain rippling through me.

Instead of focusing on the pictures of my younger self decorating the walls, I drifted into Mom's room. Her bed took up most of the space, the sheets tucked in crisp and tidy and its huge purple comforter pulled down as if waiting for Mom to climb in for another nap.

"What are you doing?" Denzel's voice was extra deep, almost resigned.

"Checking her schedule. If she had plans with someone, she would've written it down."

True to form, Mom's planner rested on her nightstand. The sight of her neat cursive made my stomach clench. I inhaled and pushed the air out slowly.

"Bank and book club on Monday. Doctor Jeeves on Tuesday," I read it aloud for Denzel as my gaze flitted over the page, skimming past the smaller to-dos and reminders. Maybe Doctor Jeeves would know something. At the very least, he'd be able to tell me how she'd been yesterday.

"And today?"

"Sushi with Evelyn," I whispered.

"Is that the only thing?"

"Yes."

I picked up Mom's rainbow sequined bag, which lay on its side on her dresser. "I found her purse." Nothing but some lotion; ChapStick; and Mom's wallet, with all her credit cards and cash still in place; and way too many tissues. "Nothing seems to be missing, so I don't think the door was forced open for a robbery."

"Ev."

I looked around the room again, searching for some clue, some sign that would tell me what I needed to know.

"Ev."

Something in Denzel's tone made me straighten. "What?"

He hesitated, then said, "Wasn't Jamison released for parole today?"

My breath caught, and I checked the date on my phone, though my pounding heart had already confirmed it.

"Yes," I whispered, remembering the man from the drug bust I'd put away three years ago for what should have been a long time. Unfortunately, the state had agreed to lessen his sentence in exchange for his cooperation to catch his boss, Long John. He'd sworn the day I put him away that he'd get even. I just hadn't believed it.

It could just be a coincidence. Though I'd learned better than to actually believe in chance. In my line of work, coincidences were almost always related.

The sound of tires on the street drew me back to the living room as an ambulance pulled into the driveway. "The EMTs are here," I told Denzel as I opened the door for a man and a woman, pointing them toward Mom's body, my head still reeling from the possibility of someone I'd put away murdering her.

"I'll be there soon," he said before hanging up.

To give me something to do and avoid looking at the EMTs around Mom's body, I scanned a letter on the table in the entryway—careful not to touch anything now that it really might be a crime scene. The letter talked about some changes to Mom's life insurance policy. She must've been updating it because of the cancer.

Barely a minute later, a cop car parked next to the ambulance. The next few minutes passed in a blur while I answered the officer's questions. He went to confirm Mom's death, then called the coroner.

"It's probably better if you wait outside while we finish up in here," the officer said.

"I'd rather—" I stopped as Denzel's black Toyota parked on the curb. The sight of it reminded me of Mr. Warner's earlier comment.

I darted down the driveway and cut across the neatly trimmed grass to pound on his front door. "Mr. Warner, are you home?" Of course he was home. He was always home. Not to mention, I'd just seen him twenty minutes ago.

Denzel rushed to me, his short, black curls spilling into his eyes. "What are you doing?"

"Mr. Warner mentioned someone coming through the neighborhood in a black car earlier today." My words tripped over themselves in my haste to get them out. "I need to see if he knows anything else—"

The door swung open. "Can't a man even take his evening bath in peace?" Mr. Warner glowered at me, a too-short towel wrapped around his wet, bony frame. "Besides, I'm old, not deaf. Stop pounding on my door."

"You said someone driving a black car visited Mom today, right?"

"What's with all the ruckus over there?" Mr. Warner craned his neck to see around Denzel and me, his eyes widening at the cars filling Mom's driveway. "Did Jacklyn take a spill?"

I put a hand on the door frame and took a step closer, emphasizing each word. "Did Mom have a visitor today?"

"Yes, she did. Now what happened to Jacklyn?"

"Did you see the driver?"

Mr. Warner glared at me again, then folded his arms. "If you want any more information, you'll tell me what's wrong with Jacklyn."

"She's dead, sir." Denzel placed a hand on my arm, his touch barely restraining the hundreds of questions threatening to burst from me.

Mr. Warner's entire frame deflated, his bony shoulders sinking in on themselves. "Dead?" His voice cracked.

"Can you tell me anything else about the car or its driver?" My pulse thundered in my ears as if I'd just run a marathon instead of across the lawn.

"It was a black car. I don't know what it's called. It wasn't a truck, and it wasn't a minivan. Just a car."

"What about the driver?" I asked.

"A dark-haired man came by this morning, maybe around eleven." Mr. Warner shrugged, one hand still holding his towel in place. "He was probably in his fifties? Maybe his sixties?"

My heart sank. A dark-haired man could refer to half the population, including Jamison. We needed to narrow it down. "Could you describe him to a sketch artist?"

"Possibly." Mr. Warner wrinkled his nose, making his bushy eyebrows ride up his forehead. "But it'd be easier to just give you his license plate."

Denzel barked a short, surprised laugh. "You have his license plate information?"

"Of course." Mr. Warner drew himself up indignantly. "I wrote it down because he drove over part of my lawn, and I wanted to report him to the HOA. He can't—"

"What is it?" I pulled out the small notebook that practically lived in my jacket pocket and wrote down the information he gave me while Denzel snapped a few photos of the tire prints.

"If there's anything else I can do, you just let me know." Mr. Warner sniffed and glared into the distance. "Jacklyn was a sweet lady."

"Thank you, Mr. Warner," I said. Who knew his propensity for spying through his rose bushes would come in handy one day?

As we walked back to the house, Denzel said, "Whoever was in that car was probably the last person to see your mother alive."

"You still think it was cancer?" I asked softly.

He took one of my shaking hands in his, and his brown eyes hardened. "Not unless cancer has dark hair and drives a black car."

Despite Mom's relatively quiet life, the suspects were piling up.

"Let's put out an APB for the car," I said as the coroner pulled into the driveway. "It's time to get some answers."

****

Late the next morning, I went back to the station, tired but determined. Every time I closed my eyes, I remembered the coroner coming to Mom's house, taking pictures, and asking about her medical history. I remembered the ambulance and the cold, final goodbye as she was wheeled away. I remembered the officer bagging the cups for DNA, and the unassuming letter from Mom's insurance company.

Maybe I shouldn't have come in to work—the tightness in my chest and constant nausea were proof enough of that—but I couldn't stay home and not find out what happened. Finding Mom's killer and helping in whatever small way I could was enough motivation to push through the pain and grief trying to bury me. Right now, it was the only thing keeping me on my feet.

I pushed open the door and stepped inside, the air conditioning hitting me like a wave after walking through the humidity outside.

"Evelyn." Denzel hurried over to me. "You're supposed to be home today."

I leaned into his embrace, letting his warmth wrap around me as I rested my head against his chest. "I asked the captain if I could come in to check on the case, even if I can't work it." When Denzel was silent for another moment, I asked, "What's wrong?"

"You were right. It wasn't cancer." He pulled back and gazed down at me.

"What was it?"

"Anaphylactic shock. The coroner confirmed it."

I stared at him, unable to process his words. "That doesn't make sense. The only thing she was that allergic to was penicillin."

"I remember you telling me that, so I had forensics run a chemical analysis on those cups. They worked through the night, but we got what we needed." Denzel's hand wrapped around my arm, a comforting weight, though I felt disconnected from my body. "There were traces of it on the cups in your mother's sink."

My breath caught. "But that means . . ."

"Someone who knew about her penicillin allergy killed her, which likely rules out Jamison."

"So who was the person in the black car?"

Denzel pressed his lips into a firm line, clearly hesitant to share the rest.

"Just tell me." I folded my arms across my chest as if that would keep me from falling apart.

"We traced that license plate. Someone is bringing the driver in now."

My heartbeat thudded in my ears. "Who is it?"

"Kevin Finch."

I swore.

"That's your fathe—"

"My sperm-donor," I finished, my heart racing. I would never call him my father again. Just thinking of him brought back terrible memories. I tried to keep my hands from shaking, but all I could hear in my head was his angry shouts as he came home drunk, filling the hall with the sharp, bitter scent of alcohol. All I could see was him stumbling down the hall in his shiny loafers, in a rage over nothing. All I could feel was the terror that mobbed me every night as I burrowed under my comforter, wondering if he'd come into my room—

"I thought your mom hadn't been in touch with him since you two left."

I let Denzel's soothing tone pull me from the horrendous memories and shook my head. "They haven't, that I know of, but it can't be a coincidence that he was at Mom's the day she died."

Denzel frowned. "And I suppose it isn't too far a leap to assume that he'd be aware of your mother's medical history and allergies?"

"No, it wouldn't," I murmured.

In fact, it would support the suspicion that had been growing in me all morning while I contemplated Mom's life insurance letter.

"Are you sure you want to be here for this?"

I sucked in a deep breath and did my best to still my shaking hands. "I have to see him myself and find out if it's true."

"Okay, then I'm coming with you." He threaded our fingers together. "I asked for a DNA test on those cups. I'm positive that when we get the results, we'll be able to nail your father to the scene."

We walked through the room, winding around officers who murmured their condolences to me as I tried to drown myself in the station's familiarity. The mumble of multiple conversations, the ringing of the phones, the scent of ink and coffee hanging in the air.

"Can you think of any reason he would've done this?" Denzel asked as we entered the room attached to the interrogation space. "You two leaving him hardly counts as a motive after a decade."

A lump settled in my stomach. "Actually, I can. What if Kevin was still a beneficiary of Mom's life insurance policy?"

"Surely your mother would've already removed him."

My heart felt like it was being squeezed, growing tighter and making it difficult to breathe. "She was notoriously bad about following through on annoying little details. It wouldn't surprise me to find out she hadn't changed it yet." I pulled out my phone and went to my recent calls, hitting the top number. "Let me call her insurance company one more time. I've been waiting on a call back"

The phone rang once, then a nasally voice answered, "Hello."

"Hi, this is Evelyn Parker. I called earlier to ask about the beneficiaries of my mother's life insurance policy." Grateful to have finally connected with someone again, the words rushed out.

The sound of shuffling papers came through the line. "Sorry it's taken us so long to get back to you. We have a lot of people out today," the man continued as Javier—a detective on my team—stepped into the room with us, his expression grim.

"That's okay. Did you find the information I asked for?" I tapped my foot anxiously, hoping they wouldn't ask me to confirm I was the agent for Mom's accounts again.

"I did."

Quickly, I put the call on speaker so Denzel and Javier could hear.

"It would appear your mother had two policies. One listing you as the primary beneficiary and one listing a Kevin Finch, though she was in the process of changing the beneficiary of the second policy."

Javier and Denzel exchanged hard looks.

"And would the original beneficiary have been notified of this change?" I asked.

"In this case, yes."

My heart squeezed again, but I simply swallowed and said, "Thank you. That's all I needed to know." With Mom gone, I'd never know why she waited so long to change things, but all that mattered was that she'd been trying. She always tried.

The three of us were silent for a moment after I hung up, then Denzel said, "Money is always a good motive, especially if Kevin knew she had cancer and didn't have long left. He would've needed her to die while he was still listed."

"Whether or not it was for the money, we have all the evidence we need now." Javier held up a small plastic bag. A handful of white pills rested inside. "After we matched the license plate to him, we got a warrant issued and found these in one of his coat pockets at home. We've sent one to the lab to test, but our initial research points to it being penicillin."

I stared at the innocuous pills. So it was true. Kevin had killed Mom. Despite my earlier suspicions, the thought was like a knife to the ribs, making breathing painful.

"With that, we have everything we need to put him away for life," Denzel said.

"If he was going to murder Mom, why wasn't he more careful?" I asked.

Denzel drummed his fingers on the desk. "Anaphylactic shock could cause cardiac arrest, so he might've been banking on that being deemed the cause of death. Many of the signs are the same." Denzel grinned humorlessly. "He just wasn't banking on Mr. Warner and his lawn vendetta."

"None of us were," Javier muttered.

Less than twenty minutes later, an officer led Kevin into the interrogation room.

I stared through the one-way glass into the small, stark room where Kevin sat—the man I hadn't seen in nine years. He still had the same neatly combed hair and well-groomed mustache with a bit more gray threaded through, the same piercing blue eyes I'd unfortunately inherited, now with crow's feet at the corners, and the same strong jaw.

I swallowed, trying not to let the ache in my chest tear me apart. After everything Kevin had taken from me, he had to take Mom too?

My fingers twitched with the urge to be in there myself, even though it was a bad idea. The captain was already bending the rules by letting me watch the interrogation. I definitely couldn't interact with Kevin. He had no idea I had become a detective or that I was standing on the other side of the glass.

"Wish me luck," Javier said as he walked into the hall.

"You won't need it," I told him just before the door clicked shut. Between the insurance company's confirmation about Mom's beneficiaries, the DNA at the crime scene, which I was positive would come back a match, and the pills found at Kevin's house, the verdict was as good as determined.

"I was expecting him to look more . . ." Denzel waved a hand in the air.

"Like the piece of crap he is?" I muttered.

"Something like that." Denzel's white teeth flashed in a quick grin against his darker skin. "He looks so put together and confident."

"I know. That's how he tricks everyone."

His attractive appearance hid the monster beneath.

My fingers curled into my fists against the chilled glass that left shards of ice in my stomach. That man, for better or worse, was the reason I became a detective—to make sure no one else would go through what I had, to be someone who would believe the victims when no one else would.

Javier entered the interrogation room and put a file down on the table in front of himself. "You're Jacklyn Parker's ex-husband, yes?" His gaze bore into Kevin.

"That's not how I normally identify myself, but I suppose it's accurate." Kevin shrugged and adjusted the cuff of his button-up shirt, then flashed Javier a smile. "It'd be more accurate to say I'm Jessica Stole's future husband."

My stomach dropped at his casual announcement. I'd heard from Mom, who still kept in occasional contact with her and Kevin's mutual friends, that he was engaged. I couldn't bear the thought of it, especially once I heard his fiancée had a daughter. And seeing him now proved that he hadn't changed at all.

Javier skimmed a paper from the folder. "You got divorced nine years ago, correct?"

"Yes."

Again, the memories and the guilt threatened to swallow me, but I pushed them away. Nine years ago, not long after I'd graduated from the academy, I'd finally worked up the nerve to tell Mom about Kevin's abuse . . . all of his abuse. Maybe if I'd said something sooner, she would've left him earlier.

"Then what were you doing at Evelyn's home yesterday morning?" Javier crossed his arms and stared at Kevin.

"We needed to talk." Kevin stared right back, not a single bead of sweat on his forehead. No fingers twitching at his sides. From all perspectives, he seemed like an innocent man—or a well-practiced, calculated liar.

Just because he hadn't been convicted of the things he'd done, did not make him innocent.

"About what?"

Kevin's back straightened in his chair, though his posture was already impeccable. "That's between her and me."

"Your unwillingness to cooperate makes you seem guilty."

"Guilty of what?"

"Murder."

"Slow down there. I'm not guilty of anything, least of all murder." Kevin's eyes narrowed. "I thought this was about yesterday's meeting with Jacklyn and the life insurance."

"It is." Javier paused, and the accusation he didn't say rang through the room.

Kevin straightened. "I don't appreciate what you're implying."

The two men stared at one another, neither blinking.

"Are you aware of Mrs. Parker's allergies?" Javier's voice was flat. Emotionless. But the slight wrinkle in his brow and the way his forefinger tapped against the table betrayed his inner turmoil. "You were the last person to see your ex-wife alive."

"And she was alive when I left," Kevin said through gritted teeth.

I glared at him, wishing he could feel the weight of my hatred.

"But for how long?" Javier pulled a paper from the file and slammed it on the table. "With her trying to change the beneficiary of her life insurance policy, you had every reason to want her dead."

"This is ridiculous. I'm not saying another word without a lawyer." Kevin's voice trembled slightly, the way it had when he'd pretended like he was fine when he wasn't. It often preceded the shouting.

"That's fine. I don't need a confession to prove you're guilty. I don't even need you to say anything." Javier leaned forward, palms down and fingers splayed across the table. "You had motive to kill Jacklyn Parker, and we have a witness placing you at the scene of the crime, just hours before her body was discovered."

A tear leaked from my eye, and my hand found its way into Denzel's. Kevin might've been one step ahead of the system his whole life, but finally, he'd pay for everything he'd done.

"You have no proof, and you won't find any proof because I didn't kill her." Kevin glared at Javier before pressing his lips together.

"You want proof? This penicillin was found in your coat pocket." Javier held up the plastic bag. "It looks like evidence to me."

Kevin's eyes were so round he looked ready to have an aneurism. "Those aren't mine."

Next to me, Denzel shifted. "He really is as good as you said."

"I know. It's why we never got any charges to stick." That, and the sort of abuse he inflicted didn't always leave the kind of marks people could see.

Javier shook his head and stood, his chair screeching across the floor with the movement. He waved in two officers. "Take him away."

"I'm innocent!" Kevin screamed as the two men pulled him out of the interrogation room. "I'm telling you, you've got the wrong man! I didn't hurt her!"

I watched him numbly as the officers read him his Miranda Rights.

Putting Kevin away would never make up for losing Mom, but it was a start. A start to pay for those nights of terror, the pain, the innocence he'd stolen from me. For stealing my last few months with Mom.

Denzel pulled me into a hug, and I sobbed, still unable to fully accept that Mom was gone or Kevin was finally going to be locked away in jail where he should've been years ago. If only I could've convinced everyone back then what a monster he was, maybe Mom would still be alive.

Kevin's shout of "I demand a lawyer!" rang through the room before the door slammed shut, taking away the last glimpse of his brown loafers with it.

"Go home, Ev. You need a break." Denzel rubbed his large hand up and down my back in soothing circles. "I'll swing by later to check on you and bring some dinner."

I nodded against his shirt while a slow, creeping numbness settled over me. Having found Mom's killer made it all the more real that she was really gone. There would be no more Hallmark movies at her house. No more sushi while going over cases. No more getting our nails done after a long day at work. No more anything.

I was alone.

The thought pounded through my head the entire drive home. Absently, I checked the mail as I pulled into the driveway. Something routine to do to keep me from thinking.

I dumped everything on the table by the front door, then headed straight to my bathroom to draw hot water for a bath. While the tub filled, I lit a few candles, then looked through the mail, ignoring the ads and bills. A letter with my name spelled out in neat cursive caught my attention.

A letter from Mom.

My hand trembled, making the words blur. Mom must've sent it earlier. One last piece of her for me to keep.

I tore it open and pulled out the letter, my gaze sliding over the words.

Dear Evy,

I'm sorry to leave you like this. I know we should've had more time together, but I thought if I was going to die anyway, I wanted it to mean something. And once I heard about your father remarrying, I couldn't let him do to anyone else what he did to you. At least my procrastination finally came in handy for once, right?

I'm so proud of you, and I love you to the moon and back.

My knees gave out, and I stared blindly at the candle flame as all the pieces clicked into place. Mom's recent and intense questions about my cases. The distracted look she'd had in her eyes ever since the doctor told her she only had months to live. The way she'd been so resolute about not trying chemo anymore.

The letter crinkled in my hand, and the words swam in and out of focus through my tears.

Mom hadn't been worried about dying.

She'd been plotting her own murder.

Betrayal and pride. Sadness and satisfaction. A storm of conflicting emotions swirled inside me, leaving me gasping for breath.

Slowly, I rose to my feet and clutched the letter to my chest. This evidence would change everything for Kevin's trial.

I exhaled slowly and counted to ten, waiting for my hand to stop shaking while I memorized her last words, the look of her writing, and the subtle scent of her perfume wafting from the paper.

Then I held the letter over the candle, letting the flame lick at the paper until it began to curl and shrivel.

Justice would be served.

Laura M. Drake

Laura M. Drake is the youngest of five children and grew up in Arkansas before attending Brigham Young University. She graduated with a degree in Elementary Education and worked as a teacher for a few years. Then she moved to Tokyo and fell in love with writing, and she's dedicated herself to producing clean works readers of any age can enjoy. She also enjoys reading, playing ultimate frisbee and board games, and spending time with her family and friends.

Check out Laura M. Drake's other works on her website.

The Chronicles of Andar—a YA trilogy where Harry Potter meets the Last Airbender.

Japanese Hauntings—a YA series with suspense and romance that's perfect for Halloween.

Till Life Do Us Part—a paranormal romance that occurs in a world between life and death.

4

Painting the Dead

LENORE STUTZNEGGER

I stared out the window from the back seat of the luxurious Bentley and smoothed my floral skirt for the fiftieth time. Delaney Manor loomed before me in all of its South Carolinian charm. Surrounded by pine trees covered in swaying Spanish moss, the mansion dwarfed my small studio apartment by a mile.

Nerves squirmed in my gut. I couldn't believe I'd get to spend an entire weekend in such luxury. After a quick, unexpected call only last week, it'd been a wild whirlwind of paint-buying and equipment rentals on my flimsy credit line to get all the supplies to make it happen. I really needed this job before Molly, Sally and I were forced to find a cheaper place in Charleston. And I didn't think my cats would like the tiny, dirty apartments on the rough side of town.

Life as a start-up artist didn't pay much. If only someone had warned me that "starving artist" wasn't just a funny saying. Oh wait—everyone had. I prayed I could hold my blathering tongue and pretend I was some semblance of a well-bred artist, if only for the next few days.

"Pretty spectacular, huh, Miss. Dhalia?" The driver, Mr. Green, opened the door, sending in a waft of warm magnolia-scented air.

He offered a hand, which I took gratefully. He was an older gentleman, but handsome. I longed to add his deep dimples and soft green eyes to my sketchbook. But I wasn't here for him.

"You couldn't have come at a better time," he said.

"How's that?" I asked as I squinted up at the marble columns stretching around the enormous wrap-around porch. Cicadas sang all around me, and the humidity was already starting to get to my hair.

"Mr. Delaney is very sick. He wanted to get the family together for one last portrait before he passes." Mr. Green opened the back of the car to unpack my equipment.

I may have overpacked, but I was determined to be prepared.

I nodded even as I knit my eyebrows together. According to my research from, well, Google and gossip sites, Mr. Delaney was only in his early sixties. He wasn't exactly what you'd call old or sick. Was I really going to paint the very last Delaney family portrait? This would be the most important painting I'd ever been commissioned to do.

I stared at the looming manor and exquisite grounds before me and wondered again for the thousandth time this week—how did the Delaneys even know I existed? Sure, I'd recently had a painting go viral, but in the art world, I was a nobody.

"Ah, the Delaneys aren't all that intimidating." Mr. Green smiled warmly as he pulled out my carefully labeled boxes of brushes and paints. "I'm sure you'll get on with one of the three children, being near the same age and all. I think you know one of them, the youngest. Charlie?"

I blushed furiously and scrambled to quash his expectations. "No, no sir. I just follow his Instagram account. He's a bit of an artist, and I really admire his style."

"And his handsome good looks, I reckon." Mr. Green winked but carried on even as I wished to sink into the sculpted concrete driveway.

The Delaney children were all in their mid-twenties, like me, but we didn't exactly travel in the same social circles. I cleared my throat as a hawkish man in a black suit approached.

"Ah, Miss Dhalia Winters, welcome to Delaney Manor." The stern man offered me a hand. "I am Mr. Hanson, the family manager. It is my job to provide you with anything you require to make your stay comfortable."

"I—thank you so much." I brushed down my flowing skirt, which skittered in the willow-fluff wind, like a scraggly Disney princess.

"I'll show you to your room so you can settle in. I have acquired the canvas and set aside the front room for your sessions as instructed. I hope it is to your liking." Mr. Hanson led me through the giant mahogany front doors and gestured toward a stately front room.

I couldn't imagine a more perfect or intimidating space. Windows stretched the right side of the room from floor to ceiling, offering spectacular views of the large pond out front. Several stately couches and various vases laden with bursts of colorful flowers lay out in the rest of the room in a fashion straight out of a Southern Downton Abbey. Old family portraits in gilded frames and painted in a very traditional style covered the mint-green walls.

I could never paint portraits like those. My style was far looser, and I used a brighter color palette. Heat rose in my cheeks. I would never measure up as the artist to paint the final family portrait.

Why did they choose me?

Despite the grandeur, it was all so . . . quiet and still. Like the flowers themselves didn't dare draw too much attention.

"The family should all arrive by this evening and will meet you in the front room by ten o'clock tomorrow to begin the first session. Please set up any of your tools ahead of time," Mr. Hanson said.

"I will." I would need to shade the windows and bring in all of my lights.

"Dinner will be sent to your room at seven o'clock, but feel free to wander the gardens this afternoon." Mr. Hanson gestured toward the back of the house where presumably large gardens awaited wandering.

"Thank you." I swallowed down the rush of nerves that almost made me trip on the marble entryway. I was going to meet all of the Delaneys tomorrow. I was going to meet Charlie. I cleared my throat. "With five subjects, I'll need to photograph them all together first with the right lighting, then I can work on each person individually."

"They have all been notified of your method." Mr. Hanson smiled kindly and indicated I should follow him up the winding staircase that filled the large entry hall.

I couldn't help but feel like Scarlett 'O Hara as I ascended the stair-case, though my skirt billowed ever so underwhelmingly.

"Here's your room." Mr. Hanson stopped in front of the last door down the hallway. "Mr. Green has already brought up your bags. I will have a servant bring up your dinner at seven. Pull the bell string by the door to call if you are in need of anything else."

"Thank you." I flushed at my fiftieth *thank you* in as many minutes. Hopefully, I'd be more articulate with the family tomorrow. I shook my head, then led myself into the most beautiful and airy room I'd ever stood in. I spun excitedly and landed on the large four-poster bed. It felt like landing on a cloud.

After giggling for an indecent amount of time, I sobered up. This home, these people, were the very epitome of high society and old money. How would I ever measure up to their expectations? This was the biggest artistic challenge I'd ever faced, I'd have to make every moment count.

I pulled out my many lists and counted through the items one last time so I wouldn't forget, which was always a problem. I was great with faces and colors, but I forgot everything else. I'd planned every last detail this week to make sure I had everything that I needed, plus back-ups—but there was no telling what could go wrong.

In a house like that—my mother's words rang through my mind—*some-one's always watching.*

I showered and fixed my hair, then chose my lacy white dress to wear—the one my best friend and two cats helped me pick out.

I was determined to look my best, even if it was just dinner in my rooms and a short walk out to the gardens.

At 7:00 p.m. sharp, a knock sounded on my door. I opened it, expecting a servant, but a tall, blond, and wickedly handsome man stood beaming before me in a buttoned-up white shirt and dark-gray slacks. I knew his smile the instant he shot it at me. Charlie Delaney.

The Charlie Delaney.

My breath caught and my hand flew up to my chest. "Oh, you scared me!"

"Scared you?" Charlie said, his green eyes as intense as a South Carolina summer storm. "I'm mostly accustomed to dazzling, exciting, and disappointing people, not scaring them."

"No, of course not." I shook my head, my curls falling around my face. "I'd never imply that—"

Charlie's answering laugh put me at ease.

"Name's Charlie." He held out a hand.

As if I didn't know. I took his hand and thrilled at his touch. "Dhalia, but you can just call me Dolly."

"Dolly." He smiled, his dimples deepening. "I like that. Please don't feel weird about any of this." He gestured around him, indicating the immaculate house. "We're just regular people with our own problems, trust me."

I let out a strangled laugh that probably sounded like a crazed ferret.

Charlie offered his arm. "Shall I escort you to dinner?"

My heart soared, but I wrinkled my eyebrows. "I thought I was having dinner in my room."

"I'd like to take you out to the gardens for dinner instead, if that's all right," Charlie said. "It's far too stuffy up here."

"I—that would be amazing. Thank you," I somehow muttered coherently as I took his arm.

His muscles bulged under his shirt, and heat rose in my cheeks. Charlie led me down from my room, his presence filling the entire hallway. I could barely breathe. How was Charlie Delaney escorting me down to dinner in the gardens? How did he even know I existed?

Charlie leaned in conspiratorially. "Don't thank me yet. You haven't met my family."

I grimaced. Would I be meeting them all tonight? My breath caught as I imagined fumbling over my words and blushing through dinner. If I didn't have a paintbrush in hand, I was as awkward as a June bug in July.

"It's okay." Charlie laughed, probably reading the pure terror on my face. "They all have their own plans for dinner. You won't have any other Delaneys sneaking up on you tonight."

I let out a relieved breath.

"Truth is," Charlie looked down at me through incredibly long lashes.

I memorized his face, his eyes—the way the electric lights danced across his green irises.

"This portrait thing was my father's brilliant idea, but, well, I picked you for the job," he finished.

"What?" I pulled back from his arm. "How did you know about me?" Heat rose in my cheeks, and my eyes popped wide.

The Charlie Delaney chose me. Me.

Charlie ran a hand through his ridiculously beautiful blond hair as we made our way down the stairs. "I found you on Instagram and, well, you might be mad at me."

I stopped a few stairs from the bottom as he made it to the main floor, leveling out our height.

"Why?" I asked. How could I ever be mad at this big, beautiful man?

"I lied to you," Charlie confessed as he ran a hand down the back of his neck and fluffed his hair. "I've actually been talking to you for months with a fake account."

My mind whirred through the possibilities, but there was only one person who I'd been chatting with in my DM's—we'd been talking for months about art, methods, and passion for success. Only recently had we started talking about our personal lives. He'd mentioned his parents were going to get a divorce, that they'd been talking about meeting with lawyers. There'd be a major problem with the will if his father got his way.

But it couldn't be him. He'd never lie to me—

"Sam27?"

Charlie dipped his head and held out his hand again, as if introducing himself to me for the first time. "It's me. I'm Sam."

I shook my head in disbelief, my mouth hanging open. My Sam, my sweet Sam the cheerleader, he was Charlie Delaney?

"Please don't make this weird." Charlie grimaced, his cheeks flaming pink. Could he possibly be nervous to meet me as well? To expose himself? His lie? "If you didn't notice, my family has a pretty big profile, and I kinda wanted to see what it would be like to just be"—Charlie tugged on his white collared shirt and kicked at the marble floor—"just me. Y'know?"

He'd lied to me. I pulled in a deep breath and closed my eyes. "Whiskers?"

"Whiskers?" Charlie laughed. "Yes, she's real. Her favorite spot is on the front couch in the sun."

"And your favorite movie?"

"Cult classic *Isle of the Dead*!" Charlie threw his hands up. "I could never pretend to be a fake fan."

"So everything is true—" I started.

"Except for my name." Round, vulnerable green eyes peeked at me through a shock of blond curls.

I willed myself to forget the rich and fancy handsomeness that was Charlie Delaney and remember my kind friend Sam.

Charlie's wide shoulders slumped. He wouldn't look me in the eye. I might be lousy at some things, but I was pretty good at reading people, and Charlie looked—bashful. Nervous. Like he held his heart on his sleeve, and I could either squash it into a thousand pieces or give it a gentle hug.

A smile touched my lips, and impossibly, I found myself pulling Charlie—the Charlie Delaney into a hug. "I'm so happy to finally meet you."

He felt so warm and strong in my arms.

"Pleased to meet you, too, Dolly." Charlie's dimples deepened with a beaming smile as he pulled back, then his expression darkened slightly. "I'm so glad you will get to paint my family before everything changes."

I knew, by our constant string of messages that he meant his parents' divorce or maybe even his father's failing health. With the amount of money the Delaney's had, a problem with the will would be . . . very serious. I nodded, and with that, we made our way out the back door to the gardens, picking up from where we'd left off as if we were actually friends. And in a way—we were.

Could that be why Mr. Green assumed I knew Charlie? Had Charlie talked to him about me?

Dinner was a delight of laughter. We chatted excitedly deep into the night.

The next morning flew by in a blur as I set up for the first session. With the help of a servant named Rose, I covered the enormous windows and doors with white sheets, arranged the couches and accessories to evoke a lush atmosphere, then set up my camera and lighting.

It wasn't long before I stood before the entirety of the Delaney family, heart in my throat. Mr. Delaney; his wife; the twins, Violet and Henry; and Charlie.

Mr. Hanson had introduced every family member to me as they'd arrived, but it was very clear that none of them were interested in me— except for Charlie, who flashed me a winning smile. At least they'd shown up looking incredibly beautiful, all five of them decked out in outfits that could have made the cover of Forbes magazine.

Cicadas screeched outside as the family awaited instruction. I swallowed down my feelings of complete inadequacy and cleared my throat. "Right, well, I would like all of you to take a seat in this space in whatever way is most natural."

Violet, the eldest, rolled her eyes and gestured to the room. "We already are." She was now scrolling through her phone. Her twin, Henry, and mother were doing the same.

"And I'll need you all to put your phones over here." I spoke clearly, though my heart was in my throat.

Violet popped her gum, shot me a look of loathing between giant eyelashes, then called for Rose to collect the phones. I arranged the family in a scene straight out of *Pride and Prejudice*—though I preferred my *Pride and Prejudice* with zombies. Mr. Delaney and his wife were as far from each other as humanly possible until I moved them to sit side by side. They did not hold hands or speak, each inching as far away from the other as possible. The rift between the two was as obvious as the dark rings under Mr. Delaney's eyes—though someone had attempted to cover those and some red spots around his neck with makeup.

Mr. Delaney must be sicker than I realized.

Mr. Delaney scowled when I moved Charlie to stand behind him. Violet and Henry, both with lustrous brown hair, did not engage in conversation with anyone but the other. They spoke of a new client with reserve and kept their voices to conspiratorial whispers.

But as soon as I stood behind the camera, ready to take the first shots, the irritated faces of the Delaney family melted into perfect contentment—as easily as a room full of politicians.

The session continued as I adjusted a flower or hand to reflect the elegant look I was trying to achieve. Charlie's smiles of encouragement were like little morsels of bread crumbs, nurturing me through the tense process. The silence was so deafening. I made a note to bring music with me to my individual sessions.

After the photographs, I scheduled times for each of the Delaneys to sit with me. Then it was time to get to work. After sorting through the images on my computer and selecting the best photo, I set up for a weekend of painting. I laid out a large plastic tarp to cover the front room floor, then, with Rose's cheerful help, brought down my tables, canvas, and paints.

I popped my earbuds in and pulled in a deep breath as the familiar beats of Lo-Fi music filled my ears. A smile touched my lips as I applied the underpainting, then began my large sketch of the space with thinned oil paint, squinting to get the placements correct on the enormous canvas—this was what I was good at. This was what made sense.

I caught a glimpse of Charlie as a breeze ruffled the white sheets covering the doorframe. He was nestled in a giant leather chair in a sitting room with a small novel in his hands. I smiled and waved, and he smiled back.

"I read this every year I come home." He held up a well-worn novel of *Count of Monte Cristo.* "Time to see what will happen to poor Edmund . . . again."

I shared a small laugh with him, then pointed to my earbuds. "Gotta concentrate."

"Of course. Don't let me distract you from your work," Charlie said without a hint of sarcasm. As if that were possible with his handsome self just one room away. He then shimmied himself into his seat as if settling down for a long, cozy read.

I shook my head, then immersed myself in the process, studying the beautiful features of the Delaney's, but something was off. An inconsistency. It was almost as if I was looking at a blended family. Where Violet and Henry were dark and smoldering like their father, Charlie's blond curls and curved eyes tended to favor the mother's softer lines. And there was something else about Charlie's eyes, his dimples—so familiar to me somehow. As if one of his little bread crumbs had fallen just out of reach . . .

A strangled scream broke through my music like shattered glass.

The paintbrush flew from my hand, spattering crimson paint across the canvas like glittering drops of blood. I ran through the white sheets covering the door into an empty entryway. The scream sounded again —from upstairs. I bounded up the stairs, followed quickly by hawkish Mr. Hanson and Charlie into one of the bedrooms where a tray of china lay broken on the wood floor.

Rose looked up from the bed with pleading eyes to me, Charlie, and the family manager. In the bed lay Mr. Delaney.

"He-he's—" Rose started.

"Dead," Mr. Hanson finished for her with tight lips.

I stared at the man whom I'd just started painting that morning. His lips were blue and his chest lay still. He stared up into the hand-carved mahogany ceiling, his eyes glassy and void of life. Red sores peeked out from the edge of his neck, like a ring around his throat.

What would make a mark like that? Were those the marks that had been covered with makeup this morning, or were they new? It was almost as if he'd been strangled.

No. Of course not. He was sick. Charlie had told me himself that his father was very sick.

But there'd been that problem with the will—

"Father." Charlie's mouth turned down at the corners. His eyes blinked over and over, as if he couldn't quite believe what he was seeing.

The room filled with a thick silence as Mrs. Delaney walked into the room with slow, measured steps. She reached a tentative hand out to her husband and froze.

My heart hammered in my chest as I took in the scene. Sunlight streamed in through the windows. A wife stared at her dead husband, her face a mask void of feeling—as if the sight of him dead broke the part in her that felt anything. A son looked upon his dead father with tears rimming his sorrowful eyes. Shattered china shards carpeted the fine wool rug, casting sunlight upon the walls in crystal facets.

"So the cancer finally took him," Mrs. Delaney said loudly—as if convincing us, convincing herself, would make it true.

"So it would seem, Mistress." Mr. Hanson hung his head. "He was a great man."

"Rose," Mrs. Delaney called. "Tell Violet and Henry, but no word of this will leave this house until I write a statement."

"Yes, Mistress." Rose curtsied and left the room.

I pulled in a sharp breath and found my chance to leave the very private scene. I didn't want to disturb anyone, but I couldn't forget those red lines around his throat. Had the cancer done that?

"Miss Winters"—Mrs. Delaney's round eyes shot right through me —"you'll hand me your phone and wait for me in the front room, understood? We have to control all of the information that gets out. The last thing we need are the tabloids turning this into anything but what it is. A man who died of a short-lived, violent cancer."

"Y-yes. Of course." I numbly placed my phone on the bedside table and shared a quiet look with Charlie. I tried to offer a small smile of strength or sorrow or *I'm sorry*, but I think it fell flat as I turned and left the heavy room.

Hours later, after the coroner had removed the body, I sat in the front room staring at the large family portrait I would never finish. I couldn't forget Mr. Delaney's bulging eyes and blue lips—or the red lines that colored the neck of his corpse. I'd use a cobalt blue and mix it with a pastel pink to get the shade just right in a painting. That dead blue.

A shiver spiraled down my back.

Charlie knocked on the door frame, and I jumped, swallowing down the nausea of that memory. He carried in a tray of sweet tea and offered me one.

I accepted it with a timid smile. "I should be the one offering you something. I'm so sorry."

Charlie nodded, red rimming his haggard eyes as he took a sip of his tea. "I can't believe he's gone. The doctors said he had six months to a year left."

My heart ached as I took in Charlie's trembling chin.

"I guess I should be leaving soon." I smoothed down my vintage skirt and gestured to the living room covered in drapes and lights. "I can have all of this cleaned up and be out of here by the end of the day."

"No," Charlie said, eyebrows knit together. "We need this now more than ever."

"But your mother, your siblings," I said. "You'll need time—"

"We must carry on." Mrs. Delaney entered the room stiffly, her sandy-blonde hair a bit more disheveled than the last time I'd seen her. Her makeup slightly smeared. "My husband wanted this portrait of the whole family done. It was his dying wish." She tugged at the large dia-mond necklace circling her throat. "All we need now is a media frenzy.

They will always find a way to turn something even as innocent as cancer into a scandal."

How could the media turn this into anything but a cancer story? I shook my head in numb disbelief as I remembered the red that rimmed Mr. Delaney's neck. The divorce. How Mr. Delaney had fought to change the will. No one knew about those things except the family and a few loyal servants—no one, except me.

"Of course, Mother." Charlie offered his chair to his mother and stood behind her, resting a hand on her shoulder.

Their resemblance struck me like a bolt of lightning. He looked nothing like the dark, handsome man that was his father. It was in the eyes, the set of their mouths. The curve of their eyebrows. But that bright-blond hair and dimples? Those were all Charlie.

Charlie and someone else. Someone familiar somehow. Someone I'd seen just recently.

The more I looked at these two together, the more I found nothing of the man that was Mr. Delaney in Charlie's features.

I cleared the tightness from my throat and forced a smile. "I am happy to finish the portrait, ma'am. Whatever you need, just ask."

Mrs. Delaney nodded briskly and dabbed a tissue at the corner of her eye. "We need to present a united front at all costs, and this portrait will be a final show of our loyalty. Our love for each other. How we stuck together to the end."

She really wants to nail that home.

"I'll send Henry in for the first sitting." Mrs. Delaney stood and walked toward the open doorway.

"Now?" I asked, flabbergasted.

"Now." Mrs. Delaney's mouth set in a hard line. "We've always pushed on when things got hard, always endured, and we will continue to do so. The sooner you begin, the sooner you will be on your way."

"Yes, of course." I wrung my hands together. "I just hate to intrude at such a time."

"My husband is dead." Mrs. Delaney's eyes met mine with thinly-veiled venom. "You are not intruding. You are doing us a great service. One that we will treasure for decades."

I swallowed down the strange disconnect between Mrs. Delaney's kind words and her expression that spelled murder. Mrs. Delaney and Charlie left me to set up for Henry's session.

The handsome older brother entered minutes later. He offered me a weak smile as I turned on some calming music. I directed him to stand in the same manner he'd been in the photograph, though he could sit on the stool whenever he grew tired.

"This will take about two hours," I said. "Do you think you will be up for—"

"Let's just do it." Henry huffed, his cheeks growing pink. "Once Mother gets something in her head, it's better to just go along with it."

I worked in silence as Henry stood, a perfect model of decorum, though I knew from the tabloids that Henry was a bit on the ditsy side.

"I'm sorry," Henry started. "It's just—"

I smiled to myself. So Henry was the kind of person who couldn't take the silence. Painting a portrait allowed me to reach into the soul. Dig in deep. Pull out vulnerabilities. It was personal, beautiful, messy.

"He and Mom haven't been getting along, y'know, and with all this talk about him being sick? I just didn't think he'd go so soon. He's been especially hard on Charlie. Threatening to take him out of the—"

Take him out? Of what? The will? My heart sped up.

Henry's cheeks reddened as he bit his bottom lip. "You aren't supposed to know that. It's a family thing. Anyways, what's done is done. No point in dredging it all up. But I thought I'd get a chance to at least say goodbye to the old man, y'know? Figured I'd get to sit by his bedside and have some last words. I'd been working them up in my mind, thinking them through—"

And Henry carried on like that throughout the rest of the session. He was so much more talkative and animated without his moody twin sister around. I enjoyed his frankness.

I focused the longest on his hooded eyes. Brooding, dark, handsome. So much like his father's. His portrait blossomed on the canvas like an old friend.

"Thank you for allowing me to paint you, Henry." I wiped the paint from my fingers and offered Henry a handshake.

"Wow." Henry smiled, taking my hand and inspecting his portrait. "That was so much better than therapy. Thank you."

I smiled and took a sip of the diet Red Bull that Rose had brought in with my lunch. Roasted chicken BLT with a fresh garden salad, no doubt grown on the impressive grounds. I spun my brush in the turpentine to clean it and noted how opaque the liquid was.

I needed to refresh my turpentine, well, more accurately, Turpenoid. All the cleaning power to rip off paint without the unmistakably strong smell. I had to make sure to label my Turpenoid very clearly. Just looking at the mason jars of clear liquid—one could confuse it very easily with water. After sealing the glass can, I searched through my meticulously packed bags. There was no Turpenoid to be seen, and I knew I'd brought extra. Three more jars, to be precise. Maybe it was still in the car.

I made my way through a back gate and to the extensive garage full of six luxury vehicles. A few restored antique beauties stuck out like polished red toenails among the black, modern-luxury SUVs and sedans. A pair of strong legs in greasy old jeans stuck out from under an antique Porche.

"Mr. Green!" I smiled as I made my way over to the kindly driver. "Just the man I wanted to see."

"Ah, Miss Winters." Mr. Green grunted as he rolled out from under the vehicle. He wiped his greased hands down a thick canvas apron and smiled broadly, crinkling his eyes and deepening his dimples as he stood. "What brings you out here to my domain?"

"I—turpentine." I couldn't think. Couldn't speak. Realization hit me like a grease pan to the face. I knew where I'd seen those friendly round eyes before. Those dimples. The curve of the brow. The set of those lips. No one other than Charlie Delaney, himself.

Mr. Green was Charlie's biological father. I knew it like I knew my way around an art studio. Henry hinted that Mr. Delaney had been threatening to take Charlie out of the will. Had Mr. Delaney recently found out about the affair? Looking at Mr. Green now, there was no doubt in my mind that this man was Charlie's true father.

My throat closed up—the red that rimmed around Mr. Delaney's neck flashed before my eyes. Being taken out of the will . . . would that be enough to make someone kill before it got to the lawyers?

It couldn't have been Charlie. He had been reading as I painted the entire time. Would his biological father have motive? Would he expect Charlie to give him a piece of the pie?

"Miss Winters?" Mr. Green's eyebrows knit together in concern. "Are you alright?"

I pasted on a false grin and swallowed. "I'm just fine, those fumes in there were just getting to me, paint and all."

"Not much better in here!" Mr. Green offered with a hearty laugh. "But why don't I get you a seat."

With as much as the family was worried about scandal—would Mr. Delaney really write Charlie out of the will because he wasn't his biological son? From what Sam27, I mean Charlie, had told me, he'd had a very frosty relationship with his father as it was.

"Oh no, I'm fine." I fanned my face as I scanned the garage. My eyes landed on my striped canvas bag on one of the many workbenches. Even from where I stood, I could tell one of the Turpenoid mason jars was missing. My throat closed up. I turned swiftly around and made my way through the garage. "Just taking a quick walk around the property before I get back to painting again."

One foot in front of the other, I walked as naturally and quickly as I could away from the man who could've threatened and even murdered Mr. Delaney. Had there been Turpenoid in Mr. Delaney's tea? My breaths came in quick gasps as I stepped into the open air, under a large magnolia tree. I needed to tell someone. I needed to tell Charlie.

His father did not die from cancer.

He'd been murdered.

I pulled in breath after breath of sharp dogwood blossoms as my chest spasms ebbed to a slow calm. In and out. In and out—

A loud guttural scream sounded from inside the garage. A jarring crash of metal, a mighty jumble of engine parts and blunt instruments smashed onto the concrete of the garage floor with a furious clatter. I closed my eyes, praying to still my pounding heart, but I was already racing inside to find—

Mr. Green laid out on the cold concrete floor of the garage, legs askew, eyes bulging. His body surrounded by a melee of metal tools, a red ring of irritated flesh around his throat.

I blinked and stared, then blinked again. It . . . it couldn't be. Someone had killed Mr. Green. Strangled him.

I couldn't stay. The killer could be right inside the garage, waiting for a witness to quash. I grabbed hold of a large monkey wrench. All my years of watching cheesy horror movies taught me I needed to arm myself. I gripped the wrench like a lifeline as I crept behind the expensive automobiles—away from the dead man who'd been nothing but kind to me, but who I'd imagined had murdered Mr. Delaney?

But then he'd been murdered the same way! What was happening at Delaney Manor? I needed to get out of here. Now.

Snap. I winced as my foot cracked a stick in half right outside the doorway. I paused, heart in my throat as I inched along, one foot in front of the other. Maybe I could grab a pair of car keys and drive away, then . . .

Then, I'd look like the guilty killer who got away. Especially if my Turpenoid had been used in Mr. Delaney's tea.

I shook my head, trying to clear the frantic thoughts that speared my mind like serrated knives. Maybe my brain was in overdrive, but I knew I hadn't invented the two dead bodies at Delaney Manor, both with strangling-type markings—and I was in the middle of it all.

I needed to think. Needed to breathe. Needed to get my phone from Mrs. Delaney so I could make a call. How stupid I'd been to let her take it.

I stepped around the corner of the garage, watching my own back, and walked straight into a hard wall of large man. I screamed and almost swung my monkey wrench, but one glance at the shock of blond hair told me it was Charlie.

"Dolly?" He cried as he backed away from me, hands in the air. "What's happened? I heard a loud scream from the garage and—"

"You didn't do it, did you, Charlie?" I pointed the monkey wrench straight at Charlie's heaving chest.

"Do what?"

"Someone killed him." I gulped. "Killed Mr. Green! H-he's dead, and he looks strangled and the killer is out there somewhere and—" I shook my head. *And Mr. Green is your father.* No. I wouldn't tell him like that. He didn't deserve to be told this way.

"Wait." Charlie held his hands up high in surrender. "You said Mr. Green is dead?"

I nodded, my chin trembling. I pulled in a calming breath. I'd seen enough horror movies to know that steeling my nerves was just as important as obtaining a strong weapon.

Charlie walked into the garage and inspected his driver, his biological father, with a furtive brow as I stood at the door, monkey wrench at the ready. Heart in my throat. Charlie's own chin trembled as he took in the older man.

"He was"—Charlie swallowed down a swelling emotion—"Well, he meant a lot to me. Was there for me more than my own father, Mr. Green."

"Someone choked him to death," I said. "See the red around his throat? It's the same as I saw on your father."

Charlie's head shot up, and he fixed me with an intense green stare. "You're saying someone murdered my father?"

I nodded, gripping the monkey wrench firmly, shooting assessing looks around my perimeter. "I know what I saw, and he looked just like this. Red lines around his neck."

Unless my Turpenoid had been used, too?

Charlie's cheeks flushed, and he shook his head. "We need to call the police. Do you have your phone?"

"No, your mother took mine so I wouldn't leak any family secrets." I didn't hide the sarcasm dripping from my voice.

"Same here." Charlie scrubbed his hand down his face. "My father . . . Mr. Green. I can't believe they're both gone. Just like that."

"We need to call the police. Now." I turned from Charlie and his dead driver—father—and stomped toward the house.

I was going to march right up to Mrs. Delaney and insist I get my phone back. Then I was going to expose the true criminal for what they'd done. I knew who it was as sure as I knew this beautiful mansion was just a façade, hiding a lifetime of secrets and decay.

Charlie caught up to me soon after, and we walked through the swirling honeysuckle breeze. Too beautiful, too sweet for such a moment. My hair flew about my head like a wild banner, but I didn't care. I knew exactly what had happened, and I knew it because I was an artist. A painter. An observer of faces. What they revealed and what they hid from view.

I yanked open the front door to overhear Violet and her twin arguing in the front room with their mother. Perfect. I stomped into the room as the white sheets billowed in the warm breeze wafting in from the open front door.

"Will you shut that door!" Mrs. Delaney growled, fingers pinching between her eyes as if she were exhausted. As she should be. Everything around her was falling apart.

"I need my phone, Mrs. Delaney." I held out my hand expectantly.

Mrs. Delaney's eyes stared at my outstretched hand with a twitching lip.

"Now," I insisted. "I have a murder to report."

"A murder?" Henry blurted out. "What do you mean, Dolly. A murder?"

"Yes." I stared down at the blonde-haired woman. Into her icy cold eyes. "Two murders."

"Two?" Violet erupted. "Are you insane?"

"Mr. Green is dead," Charlie said with lowered eyes.

"The driver?" Violet said as if she could barely remember anything about the man who'd driven her everywhere for her entire life.

But I wasn't looking at her. I was staring at the mother. Her cold eyes flashed with just the exact emotions I was waiting for.

Regret. Sorrow. Loss.

The feelings she didn't exhibit when she'd learned of her own husband's death.

"Your husband never paid attention to the help, but you did." I stared straight at the prim, curvy woman. "You fell in love with one. Had an affair. One that resulted in your last pregnancy." I paused, turning toward Charlie. "One that resulted in Charlie."

Violet and Henry gasped. Charlie flinched. But Mrs. Delaney only pursed her lips. I could tell by the look on her face that I was right.

"Mr. Delaney hardly loved Charlie, but must have recently started to notice just how much his son resembled the lowly driver," I continued. "With the knowledge that Charlie was not his own son, your husband worked to get him removed from the will."

"What is this?" Violet scoffed indignantly. "Our little nobody artist is going to act like some kind of backwoods detective?"

Mrs. Delaney's eyebrows knit together.

Got her, but I wasn't done yet. "It's clear that you favor Charlie over your other children. You'd never allow him to be removed from the will. So you did what you had to do. You killed your husband before he had the chance to change it."

"What?" Charlie shot out in exasperation.

I continued. "You did it to protect Charlie."

Mrs. Delaney raised a manicured eyebrow and smiled slowly. "I wish I could take credit for the death of my husband, Miss Winters. I really do. Because you are right. I did wish him dead. He wanted Charlie out of the will, and—"

"Mother?" Charlie asked, dumbstruck.

"Yes, honey. He wanted you out of the will, but I could never kill him. I could never kill anyone." Mrs. Delaney frowned and twisted her fingers in her lap.

A silence filled the mansion with sharp fingernails trailing down my back. Mrs. Delaney was a hateful woman who had the motive to kill her husband, but on her face I read no lies. She was telling the truth.

I stood on shaking legs.

"And Mr. Green?" Hurt flashed in Charlie's storm-green eyes. "He was my . . . father?"

Mrs. Delaney lifted a pleading look to her son. "It wasn't planned. None of it was. But by the time the twins were born, your father had grown so cold, so distant—"

Charlie shook his head, mouth agape, "I can't. I can't believe what I'm hearing."

Crickets sang along with a gust of wind that sent the bed sheets billowing through the room. The sun set a dark orange as twilight settled outside the manor. Fog rising from the warm grass and foliage in waves.

"Way to go, Miss Nobody. Anything else you want to throw at us while we're all still grieving my father's death?" Violet snapped through the silence like a toothy crocodile.

"I—" I shook my head, heat creeping through my neck. "I just—"

A white sheet rustled, and Mr. Green ambled in. The very dead Mr. Green. A violent shriek spilt open the thick silence of the night. Blood burst from the side of Violet's shoulder where the corpse of Mr. Green bit down on her delicate white neck with a throaty gurgle.

Mr. Green was back from the dead.

A twisted Mr. Green tore through Violet's flesh like thin cotton. Violet's scream of horror echoed through the mansion, followed by the piercing cries of everyone else. Henry grabbed a porcelain flower vase and smashed the undead Mr. Green over the head with it, sending him sprawling to the Carrara marble floors.

Violet fell to her knees, coughing and wheezing, trace red lines etching into the white of her neck right before my eyes. The same lines I'd seen on both Mr. Delaney and Green.

An unearthly hiss released from Mr. Green's rattling throat. His flesh hung from his frame like drooping wet clothes on a clothesline. He jumped from the floor and ran for his next victim, Charlie, whose eyes flew wide with disbelief and terror. "Y-you're alive?"

But I saw the places Mr. Green's face cracked and bled. I'd seen enough walking dead movies to know what this was. Mr. Green stalked closer toward Charlie without a trace of recognition. No feeling in his eyes but the undead lust for flesh and blood.

I let out a wild cry and ran toward the old driver—then bashed Mr. Green's head in with my monkey wrench. Blood sprayed over the hanging white sheets and prim linen couch in a jagged arch. Mr. Green fell still to the ground.

"You have to go for the brains," I said to Charlie's wide eyes and gaping mouth. I promptly pointed my bloodied monkey wrench toward Mrs. Delaney. "Phone, now. Please."

She shook her head in disbelief, her face flushed white with horror. She pulled out the collection of phones she kept in the purse at her side with quaking hands. "Nothing can be said about this. We need to keep this quiet. We need to—"

"Shut up, Mother," Charlie ground out through clenched teeth.

Henry pressed a torn white sheet to his sister's neck to staunch the bleeding while Charlie and I grabbed our phones. My phone buzzed with unending messages from my best friend, my mother, Twitter, Instagram, the news.

Are you safe, Doll?

Where are you?

My building is on fire.

The cats are safe. I set them free, but I don't know how much longer I can stay.

Be safe.

I love you.

Dad is okay. We're safe in our farmhouse upstate. Find us there. We'll wait for you.

The constant stream of news alerts read:

OUTBREAK OF THE UNDEAD. RED LINES: FIRST SIGN OF INFECTION. UNDEAD DRINK BLOOD. KILL ANY YOU FIND. FIND SHELTER. STAY INSIDE. DO NOT LET ANYONE IN.

Images of cities burning, violent undead running through the streets. Screaming. Riots. Looting. It all flashed on my screen in a torrent of unlawful Armageddon.

The phone shook in my hands as Henry let out a gasp.

"S-she's unconscious, I think." Henry nodded toward his twin. "Maybe she just needs rest, maybe—"

"It's too late for her," Charlie said, his hands steady as the light from his phone lit up the determined look in his eyes. "See the red lines on her neck? It's the first sign of this outbreak. This is what killed Dad, what killed Mr. Green. She's one of them now. We have to leave her behind. We have to go."

"Go?" Henry cried, cradling his twin's unresponsive head. "And leave her?"

"She's dead," I agreed. "We have to stop her from turning."

"What?" Henry shook his head. "Kill her again?"

I swallowed down the bile that rose in my throat. "You have to go for the brains . . . usually."

"Don't you touch her!" Henry's hands shook.

"Then we have to go before she turns." Charlie hung his head.

"Where?" Tears filled Henry's eyes as he pressed Violet's body into his own. "I can't leave Violet. She's my other half."

But Violet began to shake and moan, her body creaking and twisting in his loving grasp.

"We gotta go now!" I yelled as I raised my monkey wrench aloft. "Push her off you, Henry. Run!"

But Violet twisted, mouth open, white teeth gleaming in the dim electric lights. Too beautiful, too white to be so covered in scarlet blood.

"Henry, run!" Mrs. Delaney cried as she ran across the room, falling onto Violet. Shielding her son from Violet's twisting form. Violet snapped and bit firmly into Mrs. Delaney's forearm, chewing greedily.

A shriek of horror exploded from Mrs. Delaney, then she cried, "Run, Charlie! Run, Henry! Go! Leave me here!" The prim, curvy woman held firmly to her writhing daughter as if in a last caress.

Henry scrambled back, stunned, and stared at his mother and twin. Regret and pain etched onto his handsome face as he fell back with Charlie and me.

"I . . . I'm sorry," Henry said through wide eyes.

"Mother. Violet—" Charlie held out a hand toward them, then dropped it to his side, turning it into a fist. "We go. Now."

Charlie, Henry, and I shared a look. The look. The moment when we decided we would run. We would fight, and we would stay alive.

Rose and Mr. Hanson took in the scene through the billowing white sheets, then ran for the garage. They emerged a few minutes later in the old Bentley, pulling it right up to the front door, bursting through the front hedges in a spray of green branches.

"Y'all need a lift?" Rose called from the driver's side. Mr. Hansen's arms wrapped around his knees, his face as white as a sheet.

"We won't be too far behind. We've got a place," I stated. My parent's country house upstate. It was well-fortified and my parents had been preppers for years.

Rose and I shared one last nod, then she sped up through the grounds of Delaney Manor, tires digging into the lawn—leaving only lines in the mud behind.

Charlie and I ran to the pantry and dumped as much beef jerky, granola bars, water bottles and protein powder in as many tote bags as we could find. We collected a few knives and a shovel—anything that could be used as a weapon. Neither son knew the code to the gun safe, so we left those behind. Henry was happy to get ahold of his father's prize Louisville Slugger, signed by Ken Griffey Jr.

"This'll stop 'em." Henry spun the baseball bat in his hands.

As Charlie and I worked, Henry threw gasoline over the bottom floor of Delaney Manor, his eyebrows set in concentration. Henry dropped a flaming match on the front landing and the whole estate went up in flames. The beginning of the family portrait curled and twisted as the flames devoured the oil paints.

Let it all burn.

Charlie, Henry, and I hopped into the gassed-up SUV and sped away from the grandeur that was Delaney Manor.

None of us looked back.

Lenore Stutznegger

Lenore grew up running barefoot in the woods of Virginia with a dog at her side, five crazy siblings, and creative parents. She learned from a young age to hone her talents in art and trust in her voice. She graduated from Brigham Young University in Fine Art. She now resides in Northern California with her dreamy husband, four spirited children, a pug, two cats, and backyard chickens in a new kind of crazy paradise.

Lenore loves all things fantastical–from wizards to shark and alien movies. Supernatural and humor play equal parts in everything she writes.

Lenore's other works include: Blue Shadows Fall, YA Fantasy.

Visit Lenore at www.lenorestutz.com

5

Space Silk

JORDAN WALLACE

Dr. Billie Thorne was an orbital entomologist, specializing in silk moths. More importantly, she was alive. But it was uncertain for how much longer that would be true. After all, she was on a space station with a killer.

A fellow astronaut was dead. Sebastian Flores, once a genius in zero-g food cultivation, was now sealed in an airtight bag to keep his body from further decomposition. Billie had found him that morning, surrounded by a cloud of his own excretions, his skin blotchy, his eyes yellowed and unblinking. That was not a natural death.

It would be three more days before they were back on Earth, three more days trapped with an unknown killer. The rocket was scheduled to launch from Earth in twenty-two hours, then it would take a day for the fresh crew to arrive and another day for the five of them, plus Sebastian, to land on Earth. Until an investigation could take place, everyone was a suspect in the eyes of ground control.

Everyone was also the next potential dead body.

Billie was in the lab she'd once shared with Sebastian. A third of the room was floor-to-ceiling lockers full of her insects and related equipment, while the rest of the room had various cabinets and miniature greenhouses full of the wide variety of food that Sebastian had researched. A few cabinets where their sides met held shared experiments on pollinators in space.

It should have been comforting there, her shrine of science, but Billie felt the cold claw of death lurking behind her.

Every glance over her shoulder made her sweat. It wasn't just anything that had killed Sebastian. It was venom. And she was the resident entomologist. If she shared her suspicions with anyone, she would become suspect number one. She chewed on the inside of her cheek. Maybe Jacques *should* know.

Yesterday, Sebastian had smiled widely as he described the meal his wife, Maria, had planned for his return: "Homemade tortillas are an entirely different food than the paper they feed us here."

She clenched her tablet tighter and wiped away her tears, careful to not let any drift off and potentially damage sensitive equipment.

Jacques cleared his throat from the corner. Goosebumps ran along her arms, unbidden. She knew he was there, trusted him with her life, but still the chill of death clung to the room.

Billie half-turned to give her attention to her boyfriend of over a decade. Jacques tilted his head to the side, his salt-and-pepper hair freshly cut short with the vacuum clippers. He looked younger in the distant light, more like the man she had originally fallen in love with. Billie's heart settled after a moment. He wasn't a threat. He couldn't be.

"Have you seen Sebastian's research?" Jacques held a tablet in his hand and glanced between it and several of the glass-fronted cabinets lit with lights to mimic sunlight.

"I know he had some kind of big breakthrough he wasn't ready to share yet." Billie turned back to her work, her throat tightening as the image of Sebastian's rigid body flashed through her mind.

She slid open a metal hatch on the wall to check on some of her silk moths that were due to emerge from their cocoons. *Focus on life instead of death.* The smooth green silk casings would then be harvested to go back to Earth with them. A specimen shuddered, preparing to break free from its casing. She had nurtured this strain for over a year, bred from a group of silkworms that had arrived at the space station fifteen years before.

A thud sounded as Jacques pushed himself against the wall to propel over to her side. He floated over until stopping himself against the opposite wall. "Not just a big breakthrough. Revolutionary. He's growing crops without soil or external water. Just injecting nutrients and water directly into the roots. Air plants, all of them."

"What?" Billie peered over at the tablet, then frowned at the nutrient levels plotted out, the line over time trended downward. "These numbers don't make sense. Plants can't survive with those nitrogen and oxygen levels. He wasn't succeeding."

Jacques huffed and shoved off, back to the other side of the room.

She rolled her shoulders back as a dark-green cocoon shook briefly. A small moth head appeared through a hole. It broke out the remainder of the way, its wings still wet and floppy. The silk moth's wings would dry and harden soon, allowing the creature a brief few days of life. She charted the moth's data into her tablet as a mechanical arm reached out to harvest the freshly emptied cocoon. The silk from the cocoons was already earmarked for medical equipment research on Earth, due to its significantly higher-than-average tensile strength, even when harvested after the moths hatched.

"Numbers be damned, Billie. Look at these plants." Jacques said sharply from across the room, insistent.

She closed the hatch and pushed herself across the room. Fresh tears threatened to emerge, but she took a shuddering breath and willed them away. She fingered a bracelet, small moths woven into the fibers, a gift from Maria years ago.

Jacques pointed at three different lit greenhouses. "Bell peppers. Peanuts. Lettuce. No soil, no water. They're growing."

The peppers were bright yellow and shiny, the peanuts were perfectly brown, and the heads of lettuce were crisp and vibrant, all floating in the middle of their enclosures without any soil. Billie pushed a button and opened the hatch with the peppers. She grabbed a plant with exposed white roots, a thick green stalk, and bulbous fruit hanging from the sides.

"He did it," she whispered, turning the plant over in her hands. The peppers were firm and visibly healthy. She put it back and closed the window.

Jacques rubbed the bridge of his nose. "This could change the way we grow food here and on Earth."

"So why does the data say that he failed?" Billie double-checked the chart on the tablet—the decline in plant health was obvious with the negative slope.

"He could have input the numbers incorrectly." He pressed a few buttons and a needle popped out of the wall in the bell pepper greenhouse. He manipulated it with a control stick, moving it to pierce the plant and gather a sample.

Billie leaned her head against the wall, wishing she could just ask Sebastian, wishing he was still alive. "Why would someone kill him? He was brilliant and kind, and we've all known him for years." The next words caught in her throat, unspoken. *Why would someone kill him with venom? And how will anyone believe that it wasn't me?*

Jacques manipulated a needle toward the peanut plant. "That has bothered me as well. We've had the same six-person crew for at least the last twelve years, half of that time being spent together here on the space station during our rotations. I don't think any of us are capable of murder."

She squeezed her eyes shut against the thoughts of her friends killing Sebastian in his sleep. "It's not either of us." A twinge in her heart reminded her that she didn't *know* that Jacques didn't murder Sebastian, she just *believed* it. Their sleeping pods were adjoined, but he could have slipped out during the night without her notice. "Fedor assembled the crew and has led us since day one, no way would he kill a part of his 'space family.' Annette is kind-hearted and was so close with Sebastian and his wife Maria. Hell, Toma donated a kidney to Maria four years ago. Not one of us could have done this."

Silence stretched between them. If it wasn't one of them, it was Sebastian himself who had ended his life. That just returned her back to the how and the why of the venom. Billie didn't keep venomous species on the station, so it wasn't ease of access. It had to have been planned.

"I know what you're thinking Billie, and you're wrong. Flores just made the largest discovery in food production in the last century. He wouldn't remove himself from the world before seeing it through." Jacques reached out and squeezed her arm. His light-blue eyes were red at the edges, evidence of his own strain and sorrow. Since waking that morning and learning of Sebastian's death, everything had been impossibly sad and terrifying.

The station director, Fedor Balandin, had separated the crew into two groups to finish various preparations for the station handover and their return to Earth. Fedor, Annette Chen, and Toma Katsuki were grouped together, inventorying supplies and packing. Jacques was a generalist, so it made sense to have him close out Sebastian's research, with Billie wrapping up her own work. It was unspoken, but the lines were also drawn for safety. The three were safest, one murderer wouldn't go after two people. Billie and Jacques took on the biggest risk being alone, but as they were partners in life, they trusted each other.

Jacques's tablet dinged. "Results."

At the same time, the wall-mounted computer lit up. "Hourly check-in." The face of Zelda Young, the IT-intern assigned the check-in task appeared. She twirled one of her long braids between two fingers, her silver eyebrow piercing glinting in whatever artificial light she was under. Her eyes darted across the screen. "Anything to report?"

Billie opened her mouth to speak, but Jacques spoke first. "Nothing since the last hour. Just wrapping up research for the next team."

Billie narrowed her eyes at him, but he shook his head slightly. She turned back to Zelda. "Any news on the rocket launch?"

Zelda glanced to the side—off screen. "Looks like they're still planning on the launch in about twenty-four hours. The weather is holding. Anything you need from ground control in the next hour?"

"Any information from the security video around Sebastian's quarters?" Billie asked, biting her lip. She both wanted to know and didn't want to know. Everything was a hypothesis for now. Evidence would move the investigation closer to fact, the fact that a friend was a murderer.

She shook her head. "Unfortunately—" The screen froze, Zelda's face shifting to a jagged set of pixels. Then the screen went black.

Billie pushed herself over and tapped the monitor, trying to jostle it back to life. "Is the audio still working?"

No response.

The omnipresent buzz of computers ended as the systems finished shutting down.

"Tablets are off too." Jacques's voice shook.

She checked hers, also black. She pushed herself back to Jacques and hooked her arm in his. Her heart pounded in her ears. If another murder happened, they would have no way of communicating with ground control. Or with the rest of the crew.

Jacques lowered his face to hers. He whispered, "I think the data was tampered with. I had a look at the bell pepper sample and the levels were normal, healthy. Not what was recorded before."

A shiver ran down her back. She pressed her forehead into Jacques. He smelled like that dreadful eucalyptus soap they had on the station. In that moment, she ached for home more than she had before. "I think it was venom. What killed him, that is," she whispered back.

Jacques tensed, his whole body freezing. "Billie—"

She shook her head. "I know. *I know.* Just don't tell anyone else yet. They'll all think it was me. But I couldn't." She choked and a sob burst from her throat. Shivers ran down her arms. "We can't stay here though. If communications are down, we're safer all staying together."

"Billie, if we leave, Sebastian's research might get further tampered with. Destroyed even."

"If we're all together, we can make sure no one goes off alone to do that. We just need to stay together for the next forty-six hours until the rocket arrives. That's the best we can do to protect everything and everyone. I'll bring up the venom eventually. Just not yet." She didn't want to shift the focus away from the real killer by becoming the number one suspect.

Jacques tucked the tablet into the back of his belt. He pulled her into an embrace.

Everything felt wrong: Her body shook. Her heart thundered. Her breath stuttered. But she knew it was their best option.

Jacques nodded. "I love you, Billie. Whatever happens next, never forget that."

* * *

"Priority is getting communications functioning." Fedor scratched the top of his head, where a jagged scar cut through his thick brown hair and extended down his forehead.

They had gathered in the mess hall, the five of them, for the easy access to food and supplies—and no way to sneak off alone. All of the computer monitors were dark, their usual background beeps and clicks silent.

"Problem with ground control?" Toma Katsuki muttered from the corner, his eyes shut. He was like a cat, needing frequent naps.

Fedor grunted. "Could be a problem here. Won't know 'til we investigate."

Billie watched each of her companions with a wary eye. And she hated doing it. Fedor was managing the crisis beautifully, as he always did—with a steady confidence. Annette was scrounging food from the cabinets, attempting to make a cohesive feast with what remained of their dwindling supplies. Katsuki's resting was familiar, a sense of normalcy Billie hadn't felt in the previous eight hours.

When they met up with the rest of the crew, Jacques distanced himself from her. They didn't want to appear too nervous in front of the others. Despite knowing that Sebastian's work was sabotaged, they didn't know who had done it. And alienating everyone else wouldn't help them find out.

Additionally, if anyone else discovered venom killed Sebastian, Billie didn't want Jacques to be an implied co-conspirator.

Jacques tugged a computer free from the wall and checked the cables. "I don't think we're going to find anything internally. Not with all of the systems down."

Billie pulled a manual from the wall, *Emergency Protocols*. She flipped to the back, where various schematics were stored. She found the one she needed, and pushed herself through the micro-gravity over to Fedor. She pointed to a diagram of panels on the exterior of the station. "This is our best bet. External power and communications ports. Maybe some connection got loose or a cable froze through."

Katsuki yawned and unclipped from the corner to float over. "You're proposing a spacewalk when there's a murderer about *and* we have no communication with Earth?"

"Toma." Fedor's voice darkened, a threatening reminder of his military past. "We know each other. We are family here. Whatever happened to Sebastian, no murderer here."

Katsuki pulled at the flowing black hair near his neck. "Family members can be murderers too. Denying it doesn't help anyone. And, yes, it was a murder. Security systems were down for three and a half hours last night. Around the time Sebastian died."

Billie bit the inside of her cheek as Fedor's face reddened and his hands tightened into fists.

Fedor relented and shook his head. "Billie's plan is the best we have. We'll send two on a spacewalk, and keep the other three here."

Annette cleared her throat, arms full of rations. "But first, we eat. I must insist." Her red cat-eye glasses framed her soft face and gave her a sense of style that was hard to find on the space station when everyone was in navy-blue sweats.

They slurped food from pouches in near silence, an abnormal experience for them. Usually, meals were full of sharing science and reminiscing. After a few minutes of quiet, Annette tried to break the spell. "Does anyone have plans for next year? On our leave?"

Billie glanced at Jacques. He kept his eyes down. They had talked about getting married, but neither of them had planned anything. Now, thinking about a wedding when Sebastian was dead seemed wrong.

Annette rubbed her fingers along a thin gold chain necklace. "Last year, I spent the summer in South America, with"—her voice caught—"with Sebastian and his wife. We were going to—"

"I'm going to help Maria plan the funeral." Katsuki's voice cut through Annette's faltering words. He looked each of them in the eyes.

Billie nodded slowly and the rest followed suit. Annette cried, holding a cloth to her face to catch any stray liquid. Fedor sniffed and rubbed his face. They finished the meal with only the quiet beeping of background systems.

"Toma. Billie. You do the spacewalk." Fedor pointed at them without discussion.

Billie pulled at the edges of her shirt; her stomach clenched in knots. She didn't want to leave Jacques. Didn't want to be isolated with someone else. The thought of being alone with Katsuki in the cold of space had her questioning how much she trusted him. She swallowed her nerves. This was just another thing she had to do to survive and move on to the next day. Getting communications up was a priority. Over everything.

"Why them?" Jacques folded his arms and leveled the question at Fedor.

"Toma is most experienced with spacewalks. Billie is most adept at maneuvering tools for repairs. You have better candidates in mind?" Fedor's gaze was even, his logic unquestionable.

Seventy-nine minutes later, Billie found herself strapped in a space suit next to Katsuki, but he had one additional piece to his suit. After a fault on one of their emergency manual jetpacks, there was only one pack left, and Katsuki was more experienced with maneuvering it. They weren't supposed to go on another spacewalk before the replacement arrived on the next rocket. The other three astronauts were a blur around her, fussing with cords and tubes and checking oxygen levels. She didn't know who cleared her to exit. It took everything in her to not vomit from the unease. She only heard the okay as the others moved behind the airlock to allow the room to depressurize.

Space was brilliant and shocking every single time Billie found herself in it. It was easy to be lulled into normalcy on the station, but outside, she was confronted with the unending power and majesty that was space. Earth shone bright and blue. The sun's deadly rays were blocked with her helmet, but its light was still there. True black, something she'd never seen anywhere other than in space, stretched on forever and ever.

Billie grasped the rungs of the ladder that stretched sideways along the station, following behind Katsuki. Her breath echoed in her helmet. That, along with the fast *thud, thud, thud* of her heartbeat, was all she could hear. No fuzz of the communicator, no instructions from those inside, no warnings from her companion. The danger of the situation hit her, and her hands froze, fingers refusing to release the metal holds that held her safely to the space station.

She sucked in a breath and turned, her vision partially obscured by her helmet. A thick safety cable stretched from her suit back to the entrance portal, Katsuki's drifting next to hers. Safe. This was all routine. All safe.

When they arrived at the access hatch, Katsuki pried it loose with the crowbar tethered to his waist. Billie scanned the inside, comparing it with her mental map of the hatch's contents, she let out a breath when she found the correct communication wires. A glance back at Katsuki showed he was watching her closely.

She swallowed back a lump in her throat. He didn't trust her. Was there even anything she could tell him—if communications were functioning—that would change his mind? That Sebastian was her closest collaborator? That she had cried with Maria the year they'd both lost pregnancies?

It wouldn't be enough to keep that look of betrayal from his face.

All of the wires were intact. And the panel lights indicated all of the lines held power. She ran a gloved hand along each line to feel for unseen abnormalities, but none existed. She pointed out the correct wires to Katsuki for him to check as well.

Fedor didn't want to admit any of them were murderers. Which was suspect, but also very *him.* They were his space family, his children. It would be hard to fit that world view with someone being a killer. But would it be difficult to fit that world view with being a killer? Family members could still kill each other.

The random feast of noodles and stew pouches from earlier turned over in her stomach. Fedor couldn't have killed Sebastian. There was no way.

Katsuki gave a thumbs up and motioned for her to seal the hatch back up. Once everything was secure, Billie led the way back to the station entrance. Her hands stiffened with each movement. Was Jacques still alive? Was anyone?

Why couldn't she staunchly believe in everyone like Fedor did?

Her hand slipped on the third-to-last rung. Reflexively, she grabbed onto the stabilizing cable. Instead of pulling tight as a lifeline between her and the station entrance, it drifted weakly in her grip. "Shit." The curse echoed in her helmet with nowhere else to go.

Her heart thundered, and sweat slicked her skin, making everything in her space suit clammy. Her right hand, tightly gripped to the rung on the wall, was all that kept her from floating off into space.

And, inevitably, death.

The muscles in her fingers twitched, threatening to release. Adrenaline pumped through her. She pawed at an emergency tether at her waist but couldn't find purchase with her useless hand.

The cold expanse of space waited to welcome her, to slowly smother her noiseless screams as she suffocated and died.

She felt a push on her shoulder from behind. The shock made her right hand slip. She scrambled, trying to gain purchase on the rung as she drifted just out of reach.

Everything stilled into a dull numbness. Katsuki was going to push her away from the station. There were maybe another five hours' worth of oxygen left in her suit. Enough for her to watch as the space station moved away. Enough to stare down at Earth and weep. And everyone would just think it was an accident.

Instead, she felt a tug on her waist. A glance down revealed a tether clipped between herself and Katsuki. His eyes were wide with terror, but his jaw was set. He nodded over to the side.

Billie regained her grip on the rung and looked to where Katsuki had indicated. His safety cable also floated off to the side, not attached to the space station.

Nothing but their own hands were between them and death.

But Katsuki had saved her. He could have let her die, could have killed her, but he didn't. He held one of his hands on the jetpack trigger, ready if they were to slip from the ladder again. A handful of never-ending minutes later, Billie was close enough to open the hatch, clip them to the inside, and pull her and Katsuki to safety.

Katsuki closed and locked the hatch behind them, and they both went limp, drifting in the middle of the room as it repressurized. Billie splayed out and closed her eyes. They had been seconds from death.

Two stabilizing cables didn't just disconnect on their own. There truly was a murderer aboard.

It wasn't her. It wasn't Katsuki. Heavy guilt pressed on her chest that she had ever suspected him. He had just saved her life, risking his own in the process.

That left three.

No. It wasn't Jacques either.

That left two.

Seconds or minutes or hours passed until a loud beep signaled that the room had pressurized correctly.

Her arms shook as she twisted around and fumbled with the latches to her helmet. A shadow crossed in front of her. She pushed back, legs kicking uselessly in the air, scenarios passing through her mind of the murderer—flashing between Fedor and Annette's faces—stabbing her in the chest or strangling her.

"Billie. Love. You're safe. I'm here." Jacques's voice melted through her, like fresh coffee after a long winter night. She sagged into him and sobbed. He unlatched her helmet and pushed the hair out of her damp face. He pressed his forehead to hers. "You're safe."

"No." Her voice cracked. "No, I'm not. None of us are."

Katsuki lifted his helmet from his head as Fedor and Annette floated in. "She's right. None of us are safe anymore. Except—"

Fedor's face darkened.

Katsuki continued as he pulled off more of his space suit, hair slicked with sweat. "Except the killer."

Billie glanced between Fedor and Annette. The only people she could even slightly suspect. But in that moment, Fedor looked as he had when he told them of Sebastian's death. Utterly devastated. Harsh lines across his face added years to his age—deep lines of care and concern. A steady stream of tears leaked from Annette. She carefully dabbed each bubble of water that drifted through the room. Her face was pale, eyes wide.

Even after nearly dying in space, Billie wasn't convinced that one of them could have killed her. Or Katsuki. Or even Sebastian.

Jacques helped her pull free from the space suit. He tightly gripped her arm. "Enough waiting for the rocket and an investigation on Earth, damn it. We can't keep living in fear like this."

Everyone glanced at each other. Fedor rubbed his forehead with both hands. "How are we to investigate?"

Billie raised an eyebrow at Jacques. He nodded. "The data. Someone tampered with Sebastian's experiments. If we can figure that out, we will have our"—she swallowed sharply—"our murderer." She left out the venom. It would just make them leap to conclusions before proving anything. Conclusions that would be very bad for her.

Jacques tilted his head. Even if he disagreed with her decision to withhold information, he wouldn't interfere. "I was just at the beginning of discovering the tampering when communications went out.

Which necessitated us leaving the lab and gathering in the mess hall. Now that we're all here, let's go back to the lab and finish parsing out what happened to Sebastian's experiment."

"Won't the murderer just tamper with the evidence again while we're in there?" Katsuki closed his eyes and sighed. It was obvious he needed sleep, but Billie wondered if any of them would be sleeping until the rocket arrived.

Billie pushed her damp hair back. "Tampering with physical experiments while we're all there would be nearly impossible. We don't have access to the computers, so our information is limited at best." Limited, but possibly enough.

"To the lab, then," Fedor announced in a gruff voice as he crossed his arms over his wide chest.

Apart from Billie and Jacques who were linked arm in arm, everyone kept even distances from each other as they pulled themselves along the station to the entomology and food lab.

* * *

The lab felt small with the five of them in there, smaller still after one of them had tried to kill her less than an hour before. Billie's throat tightened as she looked at each of them. She pushed back from Jacques, needing space to slow her thundering heart. Her back bumped against the far wall, as far away from everyone as she could get in the small space. Her insects chittered and buzzed behind her, a chorus of sounds that slowed her breathing, easing her anxiety. Jacques explained the data that he'd found on the tablet before it went black.

"And we're just supposed to look at the plants here and somehow know something?" Annette tugged off her red-rimmed glasses and rubbed them on the edge of her shirt.

Katsuki opened the hatch to the peanut plant. Bunches of the legumes dangled from white roots, topped by a bushy green plant. "How does this, amazing as it is, have anything to do with Sebastian's murder?"

Jacques ran a hand through his hair. "I don't know. I've spent all day thinking about it and have come up with nothing."

Billie tapped the wall behind her. She needed something to do, something to focus on other than being in that room with a killer. The air thinned, and her mind spun. Images of floating away from the station—dying in the dark of space—flashed across her mind. The others could stare at the plants for a few minutes while she checked on her moths. They should have all hatched by then and it would give her mind something else to latch onto. If everything was going to hell, at least she could know that her moths were safe.

"Right. Since we already have the peanut plant out, let's start there. Was he allergic?" Fedor lifted the plant from Katsuki, flipped it upside down, and leaned in close to observe the peanuts.

"No. But I have heard of adults spontaneously developing food allergies. It isn't uncommon actually," Annette replied.

Billie turned and opened the hatch to the moths. Green wings fluttered about, beating sharply. She released a slow breath. They were alive.

"There it is. Anaphylaxis caused by peanuts he was growing." Fedor's deep voice boomed from behind. "None of us are killers."

She frowned as something flashed yellow behind a moth. She leaned forward to inspect the habitat closer as the weight of Fedor's words hit her. She turned and arched an eyebrow. "Wait. Then who tried to kill Toma and me?"

Fedor waved her off. "Accident."

"No. That's too much of a coincidence." Billie turned back to the moths. The yellow flashed again, with some brown. Not a moth— something that didn't belong there. She moved to the side to get a better view. A yellow scorpion twisted in the microgravity, its stinger lashing out at moths that quickly moved out of the way.

Billie hadn't brought scorpions aboard the ship. Even if she had, it never would have been a Brazilian yellow scorpion; they were incredibly dangerous. She didn't fear that danger, but she did respect it—by keeping them as far away as possible.

"Besides," Jacques interrupted her thoughts, "anaphylaxis doesn't present with yellowed eyes. My sister is allergic to shellfish; I've seen it before. While it can look different to each allergic person, Sebastian's symptoms better match poisoning."

"Venom." She spun around, her whole body buzzing, anticipating accusations. "Venom poisoning presents with those symptoms." Billie glanced at each of her companions. Who brought the scorpion aboard? And then waited a whole year before unleashing the deadly arachnid? Scorpions weren't exactly easy to sneak onto a space station.

Katsuki scoffed. "Who would bring a venomous insect aboard?"

Billie tapped the moth habitat, her skin growing hot with anger. "I would never endanger my other species, my other research, with a venomous insect. But someone did. There's a scorpion in here. A—" She bit the inside of her cheek. *Brazilian yellow scorpion.* Blood thundered in her ears.

Annette fingered her necklace with one hand and pointed with the other. She nearly shouted, "She's the entomologist. Billie. Who else would know how to kill with a bug?"

Billie glanced at the faces staring at her. She couldn't form the words to retort the accusation. She needed to think, so she let the words hang in the air. Her mind spiraled, not latching onto anything. She had to collaborate or her mind would keep filling with empty answers. "First, the data. There is a Brazilian yellow scorpion in my moth habitat. It does not belong there, and it will surely kill my moths if they get too close. Those moths are my life's work." She turned back to the habitat and pushed the buttons for the mechanical arm to isolate the scorpion.

Katsuki chimed in. "Billie couldn't have sabotaged her own stabilization cable, nor mine. And even if she had, I was the one with the jet pack, it would have been certain death to detach herself."

Annette's voice rang high. "A murder-suicide then. She couldn't live with the guilt or thought we were getting too close."

"Brazilian scorpion, you said?" Jacques directed the question to Billie, but his eyes were on Annette. Fedor and Katsuki followed his gaze.

Billie nodded as the mechanical arm pulled the deadly scorpion from her moths and deposited it into an empty habitat. Why, though? Why would Annette kill Sebastian? And try to kill her? She looked over Annette in a second, searching for guilt on her face. She looked afraid more than anything.

Annette tugged on the gold chain necklace again, a staple of her wardrobe, on and off Earth. On the station, it held a wedding ring, a safe way to store such jewelry. Billie sucked in a breath.

Annette's necklace was missing her wedding ring. And possibly had been the whole trip. Billie just hadn't noticed. "Annette. You were in South America last year, weren't you? Perhaps Brazil?"

"What do I know of bugs?" Annette's eyes darted around the room. "It has to be her. It's so obvious now."

Jacques pushed from the wall to be with Billie and tightly gripped her arm. Katsuki looked between Annette and Billie with narrowed eyes. Fedor's face reddened.

"Why aren't you wearing your ring, Annette?" Billie pushed the fear away and stopped looking around. She kept her eyes firmly on the killer.

Annette pulled off her glasses and fumbled with them in her hands. "I sent it in to get resized before the launch, and it didn't finish in time."

"You said your husband left eighteen months ago," Fedor said in a quiet voice.

"I—" Annette replaced her glasses and clenched her jaw. "Yes, Eugene and I separated. But that doesn't make me a killer."

A memory from dinner the night before flashed across Billie's mind. Sebastian talking about Maria's tortillas. Annette laughing too loudly, without much of a smile on her face. Billie's heart sank. She hated the realizations filling her head, the years of memories of glances from Annette to Sebastian that were never reciprocated. "You loved him, didn't you? Sebastian. Or at least you thought you did. Is that why you killed him? He wouldn't leave Maria for you?"

Annette slumped, the fight gone from her face. "I loved Sebastian. I have for years. I thought he loved me too. But over the summer when

I asked him to leave Maria for me, he refused. I brought the scorpion with me on a whim. After a year in space together, he had to agree to be with me. If he didn't. Well."

No one moved or said anything. A mixture of relief and anger and adrenaline pumped through Billie.

Fedor cleared his throat. "As commander of this vessel, I have the responsibility to uphold the law. Under that authority, I arrest you, Annette Chen, for the murder of Sebastian Flores." He pulled her arms behind her and held them there before looking around with a raised eyebrow. Handcuffs weren't exactly standard kit in space.

Katsuki unclipped the stabilizing tether from the corner and handed it to Fedor who wrapped it tightly around Annette's wrists.

Jacques held a hand up to his mouth, then inhaled sharply. "And the attempted murder of Billie and Toma. Why though?"

Annette pursed her lips and shook her head. "Like I said, murder-suicide. No one would look for me after Billie supposedly killed herself and left the scorpion behind as evidence."

Billie couldn't breathe. She had almost died so Annette could go free. But there was still one thing unexplained. "You had help, didn't you?" Billie pushed lightly from the wall, hazarding to get closer to her once-friend-turned-murderer. "There was nothing wrong with the exterior communications. The problem is with ground control. Maybe a co-conspirator?"

Annette shrugged, resignation written across her features. "Some intern back on Earth screwed up Sebastian's data entries and deleted the original data. Sebastian had a message drafted to send to her boss; she would have been fired. I didn't give her all the details, but Zelda agreed to hack the security cameras for me for a few hours last night so I could delete the message, or so I told her. I had her cut communications again so you could die without anyone watching and learning the truth." Her eyes burned with anger, and she lunged forward, fighting against Fedor's grip. She screamed, "Why couldn't you just die?"

The room was quiet except for Annette's heavy, angry breathing. Billie curled herself into Jacques' chest, listening to his quickened heartbeat. She had almost died. Space had almost stolen her last breath. Nothing could have brought Sebastian back, but there was small relief in knowing no one else had died by Annette's hands. And it would take work to recover from facing her death in space, but Billie would come back to the space station next year—with some new crew members— and continue her studies in Sebastian's honor.

The sad group left the lab together to head to the personal quarters, the only place to confine a killer on the station. Fedor unhooked the tether from Annette's hands and pushed her into her sleeping pod. He twisted the tether around the handle and a nearby hook. Not that he needed to bother, none of them would let her out of their sight for the thirty-odd hours left before their relief arrived. Hopefully long after communications returned.

Thirty hours and then another six to return to Earth. Then Billie could be free of the weight that had settled on her chest ever since Sebastian's death. Two life-long friends lost in one day. She shuddered.

Billie pressed herself into Jacques, and he wrapped his arms around her. "You're safe now, my love."

She nodded against his chest. "With you, always."

He pushed back from her to look at her directly. "You almost died today. And I couldn't do anything to help you."

A laugh bubbled from her, incongruous with everything else that had happened that day. "When I almost died, I thought about how horrible it would be to die alone. Let's set a date for our wedding."

He pulled her face up to his and kissed her. "The second we are back on solid ground, I am kneeling down with this." He slipped a necklace out from under his shirt, and peeled a piece of tape off that had held it to his skin. A thin wooden band floated around the chain. "But would you hold onto it for me until then?"

Billie smiled and nodded as he unclasped the necklace from around his neck and clasped it around hers instead. She ran her fingers along the polished wood. Inside the band, a line of words was engraved. *You shine brighter than all the stars. Love you to the end of space and back.*

Jordan Wallace

Jordan Wallace is an author from New Mexico where she writes with the background of pink sunsets after her children go to bed. She writes fantasy and science fiction and while this is her first publication, she hopes more of her stories will be out in the world soon. You can find more about her work on Instagram at authorjordanb.

6

The Egg House

REBECCA YOCKEY

Lydia St. Clair hadn't married Hank for his money, but she certainly didn't object to it. She waved her silk folding fan in front of her face and lifted a few blonde curls to cool her neck as she waited for their butler, Bernard, to load the luggage onto their riverboat.

For their first anniversary, her husband had planned a three-month trip downriver to a surprise destination. Sunlight glinted off the polished wood exterior of their newly purchased boat floating in the dark-green river. It had all the modern equipment, including a motor, a gracious cockpit with sofas for lounging, and a dining table.

Despite the calling birds, cicadas singing, and planned festivities, something about the morning was exceptionally calm. Hank headed down the dock toward her, carrying his bag of golf clubs. "Can't forget these darlings, can I?"

"You and your golf." Lydia smiled, rolling her eyes and folding her fan. "How ever would you survive without it?"

"You ought to try it, dear. I think you'd be a natural." Hank nudged her gently, then turned to Bernard. "So, chap, you think we're ready to head off?"

"Yes, sir." Bernard tipped his hat.

Hank had assured Lydia they'd have plenty of help at their vacation spot but insisted that Bernard come along because he was such a trusted servant. Bernard helped Lydia step into the boat. "I've prepared a light lunch of cucumber sandwiches and tea, ready below deck," he said.

As her husband steered the vessel, Lydia's eyes grew heavy. She lay down in the cockpit, leaving the windows open so the cool breeze could drift through the room as she slept. She dreamt of the ocean, beautiful and serene until a sudden squall overtook the boat. A monstrous creature arose from the depths and thrashed about in an attempt to drown her.

A sudden jolt rocked the boat, waking Lydia. Her heart raced as she blinked her eyes open. Everything in the room seemed fine, but the sky outside was now overcast, robbing the world of its vibrant colors. Egret's calls drowned out the peaceful sounds of the river. She headed onto the deck as her husband guided the boat into a small lagoon.

"It felt like we hit something." An unexpected chill ran down Lydia's spine.

Willows, moss-covered oaks, and cypress trees nearly canopied the lagoon, decreasing the light and cooling the air.

"No, just a thick patch of seaweed was all." Hank shrugged, running a hand through his sandy blond hair.

"This has to be the most remote stretch of the Mississippi I've ever seen." Lydia crossed the deck to look over the railing.

Always optimistic, Hank smiled. "You're going to love it. We'll have this beach all to ourselves."

Lydia pulled her arms around herself, suddenly wanting a shawl. He was right. There were no other signs of civilization in the area.

"There's something wrong with the water." She frowned.

It was opaque and milky like someone had dumped gallons of white paint into it. Murky water always seemed suspicious to her because anything could hide beneath it. The lagoon was a far cry from the sunny beaches and crystal-clear water Lydia had expected.

"Pete says it's normal." Hank winked at Lydia. "This is brackish water. There are some harmless white algae that grow here, and the crabs stir up the sand, making it look cloudy."

"Interesting, but I prefer clear water, myself." Lydia stopped. "Hold on. Pete? He sent us here?"

Pete and Hank had been friends since childhood, but something about Pete always left her uneasy. He had far too much money, flirted with danger and every woman he met, and didn't listen to anyone's advice. All of which might be why Hank found him so entertaining. But to Lydia, he was a walking catastrophe.

A barn owl screamed from somewhere inland.

"Yes, he's given us an anniversary gift. Look." He pointed inland as he pulled up to the dock and dropped the anchor.

An enormous house made mostly of glass and shaped like an egg, sat about fifty yards from the water. Long, green, afternoon shadows danced along the exterior walls of the secluded property. Blinding patches of sunlight reflected off the edges of the flat, connected panels.

She wondered how the thing even held itself upright. It was the most beautiful, ridiculous, and terrifying piece of architecture she'd ever seen. A small part of her fell in love immediately.

"It's like a diamond Easter egg." Her jaw dropped. "You've got to be joking. No one just gives away a house, Hank."

"No really. It's ours. The title to the whole thing is in our names. It will be a lovely summer house, don't you think?" He grinned mischievously, obviously enjoying her reaction. As sweet and charming as Hank could be, he still liked to tease her whenever he got a chance.

"I don't believe you. That's absurd." She folded her arms across her chest and raised an eyebrow.

The towering oval mansion, surrounded by Spanish moss-covered cottonwoods and willows, loomed in front of them. As she looked closer she saw that much of the interior was visible from outside, through the crystal-clear panels.

"All right, here's the story." Hank gave in, stepping close to Lydia and wrapping his arms around her waist. "A few years back, Pete bought this place for a ridiculously good price. He intended to use it as a bed-and-breakfast. But no one would ever stay in it. The locals all think it's haunted or something and scare everyone off. The taxes and upkeep were a financial drain. He offered it to me, thinking I could do something with it. Isn't it beautiful?"

"So, we are paying something for it. But that still doesn't sound right, Hank. It's stunning, but anyone who walks or sails by can see directly into the house from every side, especially at night. And since the whole thing is glass, what's to stop it from being shattered in a storm?" She shuddered as he docked the boat and Bernard climbed out onto the pier to tie it down.

"I think it's unique, and I'm sure no one's interested in spying on us." Hank shrugged.

"But it's so isolated here. It's like anything could happen and the rest of the world would never hear of it." Lydia frowned.

Although the place was extraordinary, it was far too good to be true and an inexplicable sense of danger hung in the air. The crying birds, heavy clouds, and chilly air seemed to be warning her. *You shouldn't be here.*

"Not to worry, ma'am. You won't be alone at all. Your husband's hired a staff to take good care of you," Bernard cut in as he lugged bags over the side of the boat.

"Thank you, Bernard. But don't you think this place is a little odd?" Lydia rubbed her arms. "Plus, I can't imagine it's very safe to have glass walls."

Bernard looked between Hank, who was already climbing onto the dock, and Lydia. "Well, since you ask, ma'am, I can see why folks are superstitious about it. It's not the type of place you see every day. But I'm sure it'll be just fine."

Hank chuckled. "The locals say the original owner haunts the place and knocks off anyone who tries to move in. Ridiculous, yes?" He was having too much fun at Lydia's expense. But he hadn't completely forgotten his manners as he offered his hand and helped her out of the boat. "They reinforced the glass and marble floors with solid steel beams. It's perfectly safe."

"Perhaps there's a scientific explanation for the local rumors, Hank? Maybe it is dangerous. Did any of the staff you hired have reservations about working here?" Lydia walked down the pier alongside her husband. She knew he wanted her to be overcome with excitement about owning such an extravagant summer home, but she couldn't bring herself to feign enthusiasm.

Hank ran his hand over his hair. "I don't think any of the staff were concerned. Let's see, we've got a cook, Angela. She's here from France. Though she wouldn't have heard the ghost stories. The gardener is local—don't think he's had any issues. Can't say I remember much about the maid. Of course, if you hate it, we can pass it off to someone else."

"I don't hate it. It's magnificent, but I'm afraid. Something's just off. It's like this place belongs to someone else and we're intruding." She examined the garden area.

Clearly, another person had carefully chosen everything, including the ornamental trees, shrubs, and hundreds of flowers that graced the space around the checkered grass and stone patio with wrought-iron chairs and side tables.

"So happy you've arrived safely!" someone called from the side of the lawn.

Lydia yelped, but quickly corrected herself and smiled pleasantly, turning toward a middle-aged man. He wore an old-fashioned brown gardening suit and held a straw hat in his hands. His hair was awkwardly parted down the middle, and he had a warm smile. But his eyes seemed overly confident, almost aggressive.

"Hello, I'm Lydia." She reached out her hand to shake his.

"I'm Atticus, your gardener. I'll help your butler fetch your trunks from the boat." His eyes narrowed briefly. But then he smiled and gave her a firm handshake before scuttling toward the dock.

Hank dropped the golf bag he'd been carrying onto the patio. "So you've met Atticus. I met him when I came to check the house out before our trip. Good man, you'll like him."

"Will I?" She watched the lanky figure hop into the boat near Bernard and help throw suitcases onto the dock.

Hank ignored her comment and marched up to the back door, swinging it open and gesturing for her to come inside.

She followed him inside, where obscene luxury immediately engulfed her. Sunlight spilled in from every angle, lighting up polished marble floors, Persian carpets, flawless mahogany furniture, and crystal chandeliers.

"It really is stunning." Lydia took her husband's arm, attempting to--at least sound appreciative.

"I think you'll love it here. Let me give you a tour." Hank led her through the dining area and toward the front reception area featuring a grand piano, an enormous fireplace, tufted velvet sofas, and artwork.

Lydia couldn't help but think of who might have owned these things before them. The circular imperial marble staircase led to a balcony overlooking the whole thing. For a moment, she imagined the inanimate objects questioning her presence in *their* home.

"Surely, Pete could've sold the place for millions. It's too valuable to simply give to a friend as an anniversary present." She ran her fingers along the mahogany banister as she walked past it, then stopped, standing at the piano, and leaning over to play the first few notes of *Für Elise.*

"I can't explain Pete, Lydia. He's never been one to do things by the book." Hank shrugged. "He's got interests elsewhere and probably didn't want to think about this place any longer."

She realized she was clenching the sleeve of her dress. Anyone standing near the house could easily see her every move, but she could hardly see beyond the shadows of the surrounding dense foliage. "It's not that I don't appreciate all of this, and I want to enjoy it. But it's far too perfect to not have strings attached. I'm worried that all the glitter is blinding you."

"Really now? What could be wrong?" He opened a cupboard and pulled out two glasses. "This place is a dream."

"Or a beautifully disguised nightmare," Lydia muttered and turned to see Atticus's shadow in the doorway, laden with suitcases and trunks. His unannounced presence made her jump for the second time that day.

"Nightmare, indeed." Atticus wiped his feet and crossed the threshold, interrupting their conversation without invitation. "I s'pose you don't know much about this place, ma'am? Course, I'm willing to risk it with the sum your husband offered me to work here."

"What can you tell us?" Lydia studied Atticus's face.

"Well, no one who's owned this place has stayed more 'an six months. My buddies in town say they jus' disappear. So, I'll be sleeping in the garden shed. House makes me nervous an' I don't come by after dark." Atticus raised an eyebrow at her. He was either a simple, friendly gardener, offering information, or he knew more than he was saying.

"Rubbish stories. I've heard them all. Pete owned the place. He's fine." Hank snorted.

"You've seen him recently?" Lydia couldn't stop herself from interrogating him.

"I haven't actually *seen* him. But he's written to me three times in the last month, and he sent me the deed. He's just as healthy as both of us. Enough fretting for now, dear. I know your nerves get to you. Let me show you upstairs." Hank grabbed Lydia's hand and pulled her toward the double-grand staircase.

Letters are easily forged. Lydia frowned. Arguing with Hank would be fruitless. Over the last year they'd been married, she'd learned about her husband's weaknesses. He never admitted when he was wrong. Ever.

But he was kind, generous, and full of adventure. Lydia followed him up the stairs. Behind the first door was a bedroom fit for royalty. Four large posts and thick velvet curtains concealed the bed. Mahogany furniture and oil paintings adorned the rest of the room. There was something hypnotic about the whole place, and she knew she was falling under its spell. An overwhelming sensation rushed over her—euphoria mixed with fear.

She turned to look back over the balcony. On the main floor, Atticus slowly shook his head as he conversed with Bernard in hushed tones. Something about the isolated house, hidden from the rest of the world in a swampy white lagoon, made her feel like she'd entered another dimension or crossed through a portal into the world of spirits. Her guard was up, and if Hank insisted on living in denial, she'd have to figure out what was going on by herself.

* * *

Lydia met several more servants throughout the afternoon. The French chef, Angela, came in from the side garden. Lydia came into the kitchen just as the slightly heavy-set woman was setting her baskets of produce on the counters. Angela was probably close to Lydia's mother's age with loads of graying brown curls and a prominent beauty mark. She beamed at Lydia.

"Welcome to ze house, Madam. I think you'll adore ze soup I've planned for this evening."

"Lovely to meet you, Angela. Tell me, how long have you been here?" Lydia offered her hand to shake.

"Let me think. Um, maybe two weeks," Angela said.

"And you've been comfortable?" Lydia certainly didn't want to spook the cook, so she was careful with her questions.

An expression that Lydia couldn't interpret crossed Angela's face. "Oui, Madam. I suppose it gets very quiet here, not many people around. But zee house is comfortable."

"I'm glad to hear it. Please feel welcome to speak freely with me." Lydia turned to leave and nearly ran into a woman in a maid's uniform. "Oh, goodness. And who are you?"

"Greta, housemaid, ma'am." The mousy woman, probably in her late twenties with light-brown hair and eyes, made an awkward curtsy.

"No need for formalities. I'm Lydia St. Clair. Thank you for preparing the house for our stay." Lydia couldn't decide whether the woman was simply embarrassed about running into her or something else, but she was certainly nervous about something. "I look forward to getting to know you."

"Yes, ma'am." Greta started to curtsy again but stopped herself. Then she scurried out of the kitchen.

While Hank set off with Bernard to find a spot to practice golf, Lydia elected to further explore the house and property. The interior walls were solid material painted white, with elaborate molding. The art adorning the walls verged on excessive, all sorts of oil paintings hung along the corridors, up the staircase, and beyond. She wished she knew a bit more about them. Some pieces appeared to be rather valuable.

Surely the paintings signed *Monet* couldn't be the same Monet who'd died in Paris last December. Even Pete wouldn't willingly part with those. Of course, she hadn't seen Pete in months, and neither had Hank.

She dragged her fingers along the walls, walking about the lower floor and then up the staircase. A glass corridor with marble floors encircled the upper floor. The rooms were concealed behind a white wall and closed doors. Lydia decided to try every one of them. Most of the doors opened into extra bedrooms, a few with attached parlors and powder rooms. There were also several maid's closets stacked with linens and toiletries. A few of the smaller doors, which should be servants' quarters, were locked.

I'll need to ask the maid for a key for inspections. The home didn't appear to be hiding any deep dark secrets, but being that the rooms were fairly rectangular meant there was a fair amount of unexplained space in the center. It was probably just the connection for staff passages, but Lydia needed to be sure.

As she was leaving a bedroom, she nearly ran directly into Greta again.

"Oh," she cried, then smiled. "You're certainly soft-footed, Greta."

"My apologies, ma'am. Mr. St. Clair would like you to meet him downstairs." Greta stopped herself mid-curtsy.

"Yes, but wait a minute. Have you got a key to the servants' quarters? I'd like to inspect those." Lydia said.

Greta nodded and pulled a brass key from her pocket. "This is my only copy, ma'am."

"I promise not to lose it."

At the base of the staircase, Lydia met up with Hank and Atticus as they spoke to a man who appeared to be in his late twenties or early thirties.

Hank gestured toward the new arrival. "Lydia, this is Atticus's nephew, Beau. He's going to be helping around the house—making a few repairs and helping in the garden."

"Ma'am." The handsome young man tipped his gardening hat and smiled. "I imagine you won't see much of me. Uncle A's got a mile-long list for me to work on."

Lydia shook his hand. "Well, we appreciate your help. If there are any troubles with the property, I'd like to know directly, please."

"Yes, ma'am."

It wasn't until after supper that Lydia had another moment to herself. While most of the servants were cleaning up for the evening and Hank settled into an armchair with a novel, Lydia stole away upstairs. She tried the little key in the first locked door. It proved to be nothing more than a simple bedroom. A blue-and-white patchwork quilt lay neatly spread over the wrought iron bed. A chest of drawers, armoire, and leather trunk were the only other pieces of furniture. On the rugged wood mantle sat a framed photo of Greta and several family members. Almost too innocent.

The next room was similar, except it contained a few items indicating that it was Angela's room. However, Angela had a larger wardrobe. It was locked. Though, it didn't seem reasonable to expect the servants to have to show her everything they owned.

None of the other rooms seemed suspicious, but the arrangement still couldn't account for the rather large, inaccessible area running down the center of the house.

Lydia tossed and turned, trying to sleep. Giving up, she shook Hank's arm. "Did Pete give you any blueprints for this house?"

"*Uhbffa*," Hank muttered.

"I'm asking about blueprints, Hank. Did Pete give you any?"

Hank rubbed his eyes. "All I got were his letters and the deed. I toured the house with Bernard." Then he rolled over and was lightly snoring again in seconds.

Lydia thought for a moment, her mind spinning like a dime about to topple to the floor. She shook her husband's arm one more time. "Were Pete's letters handwritten, as usual?"

"Typed." Hank yawned and slipped back into sleep.

The spinning in her mind stopped, and a pit formed in her stomach with a sudden realization.

Pete's never typed a letter in his life. I knew he wouldn't have given us this place. He might not even be alive, for all we know. So, who "gave" us his house? And why?

Lydia's dreams dizzily combined crystal palaces and luxury cracking apart and falling into the river, all while a furious maestro screamed, "This is MY house."

A rapping on her door woke her. Her head throbbed, and Hank's side of the bed was empty. "Come in," she called, pulling back the velvet bed drapes.

Greta stepped into the room. "Angela asked me to see if you would like breakfast, ma'am."

"Oh." Lydia blinked, not expecting such a commonplace question after her distressing dream. "Perhaps just some tea and toast. I'm going to be taking a trip into town."

Lydia quickly put on a simple pale-yellow summer dress and some sensible leather shoes. Then she took the path into town, determined to find someone who knew something about the house or Pete.

"You move into town recently?" a friendly older gentleman queried as he sold her a small bouquet for the dining room. "We don't get many new people in South Summerhaven."

"I'm only here for the season. We own the big egg-shaped monstrosity on the white beach." She studied him to see his reaction.

"Oh, dear." The man's face paled, and his eyes grew wide.

Despite all of her suspicions, she was still stunned by his dramatic reaction.

"I'll tell you, that place isn't right. I'd get outta there soon as possible. There's an inn here in town," he offered. "Maybe stay there."

"You don't really think it's haunted, do you?" Lydia rubbed the goosebumps on her arms, despite the warm summer air. "I don't believe in ghosts."

"Nah, the problems with that place are real. Owners all disappeared or died. The police have looked into it. No explanation. Something bad about that house." He looked at Lydia sympathetically, like he was certain her days were numbered. "Hate to see a sweet young lady go missing."

"Missing?" Lydia suddenly envisioned her body floating in the white lagoon. "What about the previous staff working there? What happened to them?" A wave of clarity washed over Lydia. She'd been right all along. Of course, the whole situation was absurd, and living in a glass house was ridiculous.

"Mostly come from other places, but different with every owner. Locals never work there." He frowned. "Well, Augusta worked there a long time ago. You could ask her. No, that's not it. She was engaged to the first owner. I think it was around 1908."

"How do I contact her?"

"She lives down Viridian Lane, just past the post office." He somberly tipped his Breton hat to her and watched as she exited the shop.

* * *

Viridian Lane was easy enough to find but locating Augusta's home proved to be a bit more difficult. The lane was hardly more than a dirt path winding through the countryside and shaded by towering cypress trees and rhododendron. Lydia's tension relaxed a little, knowing she blended into the scenery. No one was watching her.

After walking for nearly twenty minutes down the path, a cottage appeared. It was hardly more than a shack, but the tidy walkway and fresh paint gave it a charming appeal. Lydia could imagine herself being quite happy in such a place.

When she knocked, she heard someone shuffling about inside. Then the door cracked open enough to reveal the face of a middle-aged woman. Her hair was brushed up into a wild bun atop her head with rogue strands of curls landing on her shoulders.

"You lost?" she asked.

"I'm looking for Ms. Augusta Phillips." Lydia stiffened. She didn't mean to intrude, but the woman clearly wasn't interested in receiving her.

"Why's that?"

"Well . . . I." Lydia took a slow breath to calm her voice. "My husband and I may be in danger."

The woman's face softened, and Lydia realized she had lovely features.

"I'm Augusta, come on in."

The cottage reminded Lydia of something from a fairy tale with its clean, swept wooden floor, carved furniture, potted flowers in the windows, and curtains that could be closed in the evening for privacy. She wondered if Hank would ever be willing to give up their lavish lifestyle for such a perfect home. "Thank you. You have a lovely home, by the way."

Augusta looked her over before speaking. "I'm hesitant to ask what brings you to me. But I better hear it. Have a seat and tell me."

Lydia sat on a cushioned chair. "I'm told you were engaged to the first owner of my house."

Augusta's face paled, and she shook her head. "No."

"No? You weren't engaged then?" Lydia frowned and stood but sat back down when Augusta spoke.

"We were only engaged for a few months before he disappeared." Augusta's eyes glazed over, lost in the past.

"I'm so sorry to hear that. You never learned where he went?" Lydia scooted closer.

Augusta shook her head. "Heathcliff didn't leave me, I know that. I think someone killed him. He was fine one day, and the next it was like he'd never existed. Whole town was spooked. Someone new moved into the glass house. The police couldn't explain what had happened, and the new owner seemed oblivious. They purchased it through a realtor who had the deed. You shouldn't be living there." Augusta was nervously wringing her hands, her eyes brimming with tears.

"I think you know more than you realize," Lydia coaxed her. "Why do you think he was murdered? Did you interview the servants? There has to be more."

"Of course, there's more. But I was a mess—angry. And I demanded answers. When I got to the house, it was filled with people. The owner, Jones, or something, was throwing the most lavish party I've ever seen. He told me to leave or be escorted off the property. The guests were dripping with jewels and money. It was disgusting, considering he'd purchased the house for a fraction of its value." Augusta sneered and shuddered. "But Jones didn't last long either. Drown somehow, they say. He had a wife, too. No idea what happened to her."

"What was she like?"

"I don't know. French, I suppose, brunette with curls nearly as wild as mine. She was the one in charge in that marriage, I'm sure of it. I could have torn that fake beauty mark right off her face."

Lydia started. "Beauty mark? Are you sure it was fake?"

"Could've been real." Augusta shrugged.

Lydia's head spun, and dizziness threatened to knock her to the ground. "That perfectly fits the description of our chef. She's older now, of course."

Augusta looked rapidly around her house, then scurried to a chest of drawers in a corner. She opened the top drawer and pulled out a revolver.

Lydia yelped and jumped back.

"No, no, this is simply for protection." Augusta brushed off Lydia's panic. "We need to see if it's her. It's just, I always suspected she had something to do with her husband's death."

"But Angela just came from France recently." Lydia ran her hand over her face.

"Well, it won't hurt, to be sure. One thing I *inherited* from Heathcliff was a little Ford Roadster. It's around back. Hurry now." Augusta was remarkably level-headed as she tucked the revolver into the belt at her waist, but Lydia's whole body trembled as she thought about the implications.

The two women tore down the country road. Augusta was a terrible driver. She swerved into town, honking at people to get out of the way.

"I don't know what damage she could do in the few hours I've been away from the house." Lydia held onto the straw summer hat she'd worn.

When the car finally pulled up to the center of the egg house's circular driveway, Lydia climbed out and invited Augusta into the house.

Unexpected silence filled the air. Something was off. An antique vase lay shattered at the base of the stairs, and the Persian carpet was crumpled, like someone had slid something heavy across it.

"Hank!" Lydia cried out, but no one answered. She turned to Augusta, who had followed her into the house. "I don't know where my husband is. Can you please check the garden? I'll go upstairs."

"Just keep your eyes open."

Augusta disappeared out the door, and Lydia climbed the marble staircase. The carpet running down the hallway to the bedrooms had been strewn about and was pushed up against the wall.

The main bedroom looked normal, and the other rooms seemed untouched. But upon closer inspection, Lydia noticed that the door to Angela's wardrobe was open.

Lydia took a breath and approached. Her jaw dropped when she looked inside the wardrobe. It wasn't a closet at all, but a long corridor that appeared to snake through the house, with occasional little slits in the walls. Electrical lights lit the hall, but the most stunning discovery was the collection of art, vases, jewelry, and other treasures lining the walls.

Lydia followed the corridor, which led to a circular staircase. *This must be the center of the house.*

She descended the stairs, silently. The staircase had several doors at each level that must've connected to different rooms in the house. She landed in a large, dark room where even more pieces of art were stored. The items must've been stolen or smuggled because no one would give away a house full of treasures without telling the owners. Angela had to be in on the whole thing, and maybe the gardener, too. She needed to contact the police.

The room had a wooden door at one end, so Lydia tried it. When she pushed it open, she found herself in a dugout with narrow weed-covered stone stairs that led up to the garden. She closed the door behind herself and headed up the stairs. Upon reaching the garden, she looked back. The door was so overgrown with vines, she likely wouldn't have even noticed it from this side.

A shot blasted from somewhere on the property. Fear froze her in place for a moment until she pulled herself together and stole through the back door and into the kitchen.

Another shot rang out. This time, Lydia could tell it was coming from behind her, near the beach. She searched the kitchen drawers for something she could use as a weapon and grabbed a metal mallet. The stone-paved garden walkway led her directly to the back gate. From there, she saw several figures struggling with each other on the beach, and one of them lay on the ground covered in blood.

Lydia screamed and ran toward the group. Augusta and Greta wrestled over the revolver, while Beau attempted to drag Hank toward the water.

Oh, no you don't. Lydia held her tongue. Everyone had their backs turned to her. Adrenaline replaced her jittery nerves, and she tore down the beach. Her instincts took over, and she dashed Beau in the back of the knee with the mallet while plowing into Greta with all of her weight, which was, unfortunately, completely ineffective.

Two angry faces turned toward her with murder in their eyes.

Another shot rang out. This time it came from near the house. Within moments, several police officers flooded the shore and apprehended the two criminals. While everyone shuffled around her, Lydia crawled over to her husband. His left shoulder was covered in blood and he had a wound on the side of his head, but he was breathing.

"I need a doctor!" Lydia shouted at a nearby officer. Then, she lifted her husband's head into her lap. "Hank, please be all right. Why did they attack you?"

"Someone sealed Angela's wardrobe shut, so I asked Atticus for a crowbar to open the thing up. There's a passage through the house, Lydia. I guess Beau didn't want me to find it. Atticus and Bernard are . . ." Hank's voice was barely above a whisper. "They're in the shed. Greta threatened them with a gun."

"What, why?" Lydia grappled, but officers who'd come to carry Hank to the house for medical aid had already surrounded her.

"Are you all right, Lydia?" Augusta asked. She'd retrieved the revolver and tucked it away safely in her belt. "Still haven't seen your cook."

"I'm fine. But I need to go attend to Hank. Can you take an officer with you to check the shed?" Lydia asked. "Also, were you the one who called the police?"

"No," a familiar French voice spoke behind them. "It was me. I heard ze scuffling out in ze garden and couldn't believe what I saw. Greta and Beau, they've been hiding some things, it appears."

"Oh, Angela. Thank you! You saved our lives, I'm sure." Lydia paused and looked over at Augusta. "Have you two met before?"

"We haven't." Augusta reached out to shake Angela's hand. "Though you look a bit like someone I used to know."

* * *

Several days later, Lydia had enough information to put together what had happened.

The police discovered Beau's real name was Torrence Frogmore, a wanted thief. He'd presented himself to Atticus as a long-lost nephew in need of a job. Greta—really named Judith—was his wife and the first to respond to Hank's newspaper advertisement for servants.

They worked with a ring of art thieves who didn't want any legal connection to the egg house, their base of operations. The round house with glass walls made it easy for anyone to watch whatever happened inside. They silenced puppet "owners" who got in the way or discovered the truth. The criminal ring liked owners who only stayed at the house for part of the year because they would sometimes hold auctions there. Guests would come and go by boat, and the town never knew a thing about the events.

Sadly, Pete had been permanently silenced. A search party found his body and those of three other previous owners in the white lagoon.

Of course, the police removed all the stolen art from the house and began the search for the original owners. But the house legally belonged to Hank and Lydia.

"Hank." Lydia sat on the edge of the bed where her husband rested on a Sunday afternoon. "You know, there's a cottage for sale on the edge of town. It's probably the most beautiful little place I've ever seen. There is a front garden filled with hollyhocks and roses, and the back fence has a gate that opens to the woods behind the house. It would be the perfect place for a child to run and play on a summer day."

"Well, I'm done choosing houses. Do you want it for our summer home?" Hank asked, the wound on his head still wrapped in white bandages.

"I'd love it. And I want to give this glass monstrosity to Angela and Bernard. They could turn it into a proper bed-and-breakfast. Maybe you've noticed how fond they are of each other?"

"I hadn't. What about Atticus?"

"That's up to Atticus. But I imagine he still needs a place to live, and he's done a great job here." Lydia couldn't help but feel sorry for him, believing that "Beau" was actually his nephew.

"We may be the only people in history to give their home to their servants." Hank raised an eyebrow at Lydia with an impish grin spread across his face.

Lydia fell back on the bed, stared up at the ceiling, and let out a sigh. "Well, apparently, it's what you do with the egg house. Give it away."

After a moment, Hank's jaw dropped, and he sat upright. "Wait, we don't have children. Why did you mention a *child* playing in the woods?"

Lydia smiled and caressed the tiny bump on her belly. "Because our little one is going to need somewhere to play."

Rebecca Yockey

Rebecca Yockey grew up with two artists for parents, and the freedom to roam the fields and creek near her home. She is an author, editor, and teacher. Her *Magic of the Woods* fantasy series (under Rebecca Avati) is well-loved, and growing. She's an avid mystery reader. When she's not reading or writing, you'll find her teaching math, hanging out with her large family, or painting.

Find out more at www.steamengineproductions.com

7

The Professor's Death

REBECCA YOCKEY

Doctoral candidates sat around lavishly decorated round tables in the makeshift banquet hall. Proud family members, parents, and spouses gathered near them. Ambitious, sentimental energy coursed through the room.

Dr. Jorgensen, the department head, droned on from the podium about the moral obligations of psychologists. I took a moment to bask in the occasion's magic. Attending the graduation ceremony and banquet by myself didn't spoil the occasion. I'd completed my Ph.D., which was more than enough for me.

I sat toward the back of the room and had to shift in my seat to see the speakers past the floral centerpiece. As the reception wound down, I engaged in handshakes and conversations with fellow honorees and their guests, who gradually made their way out of the on-campus banquet hall into the tranquil May evening.

I lingered behind, hoping for an opportunity to express my gratitude to Dr. Jorgensen, my mentor and professor. He had not only delivered inspiring closing remarks about our achievements but had also specifically praised my research. Adjusting my tie, I traversed the room toward where he conversed with a few of our colleagues.

Upon noticing my approach, Dr. Jorgensen's face lit up. "Ah, Henry, or should I call you Dr. Webb?"

Waving off his comment, I replied, "Henry's just fine. You have a way with words, Jorgensen. There wasn't a dry eye in the audience."

Interrupting our conversation, Dr. Jorgensen's wife, Helen, said, "I'm off, Walter," as she kissed his cheek and headed toward the exit.

Helen had an elegant air about her that demanded attention, and we both watched her departure. Then, seizing a moment alone, Dr. Jorgensen moved closer to me and lowered his voice. "The speech was heartfelt because I meant every word. The world needs capable psychologists, Henry. I'm proud of you."

"Thank you." Warmth spread across my cheeks. I wasn't accustomed to such high praise.

He nodded and patted my shoulder before lowering his voice even further. "I hope you can stop by the lab tomorrow. Some of the reports Jackson submitted to me seem off, and I value your opinion."

Frowning, I expressed my concern, "I hope it's nothing serious."

Jackson, our lab assistant, had been with us for six months, and we had entrusted him with access to sensitive data.

Dr. Jorgensen wore a wise and cautious expression, hinting that he was downplaying something significant. "I doubt it's anything serious, but I prefer to be thorough. I plan on bringing him back next year, provided this gets resolved. Will I see you tomorrow morning?"

"Of course." I nodded. Clerical errors made by an intern shouldn't be cause for alarm. There was something Dr. Jorgensen wasn't disclosing.

Walking home along the tree-lined campus streets, under the cover of darkness, I savored the realization that my relentless studying, data processing, and round-the-clock work had concluded. The thought of being finished with school washed over me in waves throughout the evening, eliciting euphoric tingles down my spine. Now, nothing stood in my way.

Completing my doctorate and securing a prestigious position at a thriving psychiatric hospital would mark the end of my problems, or so I hoped. Rose-colored glasses and all that.

I slept well that night.

The following morning, sunlight spilled through my windows, waking me without the aid of an alarm clock for the first time in years. Taking my time, I prepared breakfast, indulged in a long shower, and caught up on the news before making my way to the main building of the psychology department, the same building that had hosted the graduation banquet.

Dr. Jorgensen was an early riser, and I knew I'd find him upstairs. Taking the elevator to the seventh floor, I headed down the musty hallway toward our shared labs. The door to our lab was ajar, but there was something on the floor obstructing it. Leaning on the door with all my weight, I cleared a pathway and stumbled into the office, glimpsing what had been in my way.

Jorgensen's lifeless body lay on the floor. His eyes were open, bulging, and staring at me as if frozen in an attempt to cry out. The daylight spilling in through the windows highlighted his face, creating hard shadows that exaggerated his expression. A wave of nausea washed over me.

"Help!" I screamed, rushing out of the lab and down the hall while dialing 9-1-1 The floor seemed vacant, and no one came to my aid. As dispatch answered, I tried to steady my breath.

"My name is Henry Webb. I'm at my lab . . . sorry, the psychology building on campus, seventh floor. Jorgensen, he's . . . my professor. He's dead." I gulped. "His poor family will be devastated."

Suddenly exhausted, I dropped into a chair in the corridor. After what felt like an eternity, officers and EMTs swarmed the building. Before I knew it, Jorgensen's body was being carried out on a stretcher, covered with a white sheet.

A woman who was approximately my age, appeared to be taking charge, issuing orders and directing people up and down the elevator.

Unlike the uniformed officers, she wore a black business suit. Her chocolate-brown ponytail bobbed as she hurried past me, seemingly oblivious to my presence and muttering to herself. After a moment, she looked over, her gaze fixed on me.

"Who's this?" She addressed no one in particular.

"I'm Dr. Henry Webb. I share this office with Dr. Jorgensen and a few other colleagues," I said, standing up and extending my hand, but she didn't shake it.

"So, any fingerprints we find of yours would be irrelevant," she sighed. "Why are you here on a Saturday morning?"

"Why would you care about fingerprints? I'm here because I agreed to help Dr. Jorgensen go over some paperwork. I'm the one who found him," I replied, crossing my arms.

My answer caught her off guard, and she furrowed her brow, turning to another officer. "French, you didn't tell me he's our witness. This investigation is a mess."

"Clearly," I muttered. Although I understood everyone was under immense pressure, I lacked the emotional energy to maintain politeness. "Should I come back at a more convenient time?"

She surveyed the room, her frazzled demeanor transforming into a professional façade. "Since you're already here, maybe you can provide some basic information. Let's go down to the lobby where it's less crowded."

"Of course." I followed her into the elevator, and we descended to the main floor.

"Please have a seat, Dr. . . . What was your name again?" she asked, retrieving a chair from a stack and sitting on it backward, facing me, her elbows resting on its backrest.

"Webb," I replied, sitting down on one of the black-leather sofas and staring at her.

She removed her disposable gloves, fetched a pen and notebook from her pocket, and began speaking. "I apologize for questioning you now, but given the evidence, we need to gather information quickly. This is a police investigation, after all."

"Really? He was fine at the banquet—what happened? I thought we would need EMTs, not an entire police force?" I struggled to catch my breath as thoughts raced through my mind. Dizziness overwhelmed me, followed by another wave of nausea, my breakfast churning in my stomach. I couldn't believe they suspected murder without even having performed an autopsy.

"We have to rule a few things out, is all." She broke eye contact and chewed her bottom lip. "I'm so sorry for your loss."

"He was a dear friend and my mentor. I'm sick." I shuddered.

The detective's expression softened. "Take a moment to process. We can talk at the station later if you'd prefer."

I wiped my hand over my face, wanting to escape the building and catch my breath. But prolonging things was also the last thing I wanted. I took a deep, steady breath.

"No, I'd rather get this over with."

The detective turned away from me and barked a few more orders to some officers entering the building. Then she turned back to me.

"Thank you. The sooner I gather information, the better," she said, widening her eyes as if bracing me for more bad news.

"Yes, I kind of figured that out. The police wouldn't be scouring the building if he'd clearly had a heart attack." I shook my head, staring at the floor. "Can you share any details? Officer . . . ?"

"Sophie," she replied, offering a slight smile, revealing a dimple on her right cheek. "Or Detective Ordaz. Sorry, we're just putting this together. But if you answer a few questions, you'll be free to go."

"Yeah, yeah . . . okay."

Detective Ordaz scratched a few things on her notepad. "Can you please tell me where you were last night?"

"I was here, in the main hall. They used it for our graduation banquet. Dr. Jorgensen gave an inspiring speech." I looked around the lobby, which was like any other modern collegiate building—spacious, with large windows and marble floors. "He must've stayed later because we talked for a little while after. I know he visited with other colleagues."

Ordaz nodded. "What did you two discuss?"

I paused, replaying my conversation with Jorgensen in my mind. "He congratulated me. After his wife left, he asked me to look at some paperwork our intern, Jackson, had done. It was brief. Before we chatted, I noticed him speaking to a few medical board members and department heads. He had a long conversation with Adrianna Lindor, I think. I don't know who he spoke to after I left."

Our conversation was interrupted by a fuzzy voice on her com. "Ordaz, you were right. Striations on the throat match the cord."

"Figured. Copy that," she replied, raising an eyebrow. Then she looked back at me. "And what do you know about all these people, especially his wife? Do you know her at all? How was their relationship?"

"Whoa, that's quite a leap. He always seemed happy about their marriage. They have a twenty-year-old son, Hank. But I'm sure neither had anything to do with this. Can you tell me the cause of death, at least?" I hoped to get some information. "I heard what they said on your walkie."

Detective Ordaz glanced around, ensuring no one was listening before answering. "Strangulation, maybe." She rolled her eyes slightly. "The news will probably post it online any minute. Apparently, a janitor called the local news station a bit ago without asking anyone."

"I see," I replied, rubbing my hand over my face. Using a therapeutic strategy, I imagined my emotions swirling like a tornado and locking themselves inside a metal chest. I allowed my logical thinking to kick in. "Strangulation doesn't seem premeditated. I doubt this was planned. But he wasn't the kind of guy who went around upsetting people."

"I wonder about the rest of his family. Can you shed any light on them? His son?" she continued, scribbling in her notebook.

"They're nothing remarkable. His first wife died in a fire, so Helen is his second. She's a bit younger than him. He has, well had, a son—he's an undergraduate student here—works on campus." I took a breath, trying to keep myself calm. His family had nothing to do with his murder. "I'm sure they're innocent."

Detective Ordaz leaned back against her seat, frowning. "Can you imagine who might've done this? Would Jackson have any motivation? Any other colleagues?"

"No, Jorgensen's death is going to make Jackson's life harder—it puts him out of his internship. It may have been a robbery. Or he might've witnessed a crime." My mouth had gone dry, and I dug my water bottle from my backpack. I wasn't technically a student anymore, but I still liked to carry a bag around campus.

Dr. Ordaz finished up her notes and looked up at me. She handed me a business card. "You've been helpful, Dr. Webb. I'm sure we'll talk again. Please call me if you think of anything."

I paused for a moment. "I have a doctorate in criminal psychology now, and I might be able to help. Dr. Jorgensen wasn't only a mentor to me, he was a friend." As nice as it would've been to dissociate—pretend like the whole thing had never happened—I doubted this detective would solve the case alone. She seemed to be grasping at straws.

"I'll keep that in mind." Detective Ordaz walked with me to the glass doors in front of the building. "If I have any more questions, I'll contact you."

I walked through campus back to my apartment. The sunlight glimmering through the windows made the place particularly cheery, even though most of my belongings were packed. I planned to move to the city the following week and leave this place behind forever.

But it looked like I would need to break out my textbooks one last time. It took a while to dig to the bottom of the cardboard box holding my social deviance research materials. I hoped I'd find something that might be helpful to share with Ordaz.

Obviously, I'd already mastered the topic. But there was a specific chapter that broke down the circumstances that led people to commit crimes of passion and how those criminals were eventually caught. I figured reviewing the information could be useful.

The main people the police would investigate were Dr. Jorgensen's wife, Helen; Jackson Glass; Adrianna Lindor, the department head who he'd spoken to after we talked; and maybe his son Hank. Although, I didn't suspect any of them. It was possible that the crime might end up being pinned on some lowly janitor or banquet server.

But strangulation was a crime of passion and usually committed by someone close to the victim. No one in the psych department had a reason to hurt Dr. Jorgensen, that I knew of, and no one who'd just graduated had a motive.

I found the textbook at the bottom of a cardboard box and skimmed a few lines:

Crimes of passion are often motivated by fear, rage, jealousy, financial desperation, and guilt. The victim is likely to have a close relationship with the perpetrator. Perpetrators of crimes of passion usually have prior criminal records.

It was all stuff I remembered, nothing enlightening. So, I skimmed a little farther down.

Prosecutors generally need to provide ample evidence.

Of course. They'd probably look for fingerprints on Jorgensen's neck, check the cameras, and see who was last to leave the building, or left after the approximate time of death, anyway. I had a feeling finding any evidence would be nearly impossible.

My head was spinning with possibilities when my phone rang, and BUPD showed up on the I.D.

"This is Henry." Part of me hoped they'd solved the case already—pinned it on some local criminal. But it was never that easy.

"Hi Henry, it's Detective Ordaz. You really know about criminal psychology and all that?" She sounded about a decade younger on the phone. She could've passed for a high school student if she wanted to. "I thought I'd take you up on your offer. This case, it turns out, is going to be a little more difficult than I expected. His wife and son hired lawyers and are refusing to speak to me. Since you have a personal relationship with the family, maybe you can talk to them, and get a feel for things. It wouldn't be official, but I'd appreciate whatever insight you gather."

I mulled it over for a minute. Even though I'd technically offered to help, it might not be the best thing for me to do. "Are you allowed to work with a civilian?"

"You'll be considered a witness and an informant. I'm afraid I can't pay you or anything."

"No, I don't want any money, but if I can help . . . His family is probably just used to seeking legal counsel. I doubt they were involved." I closed my textbook and went to grab my wallet and shoes.

"But why? It seems off to me."

I couldn't figure why she was asking me. She should know stuff like getting a lawyer doesn't make someone guilty.

"Well, they're wealthy. Maybe they want to protect their assets." I couldn't explain why I so desperately wanted to exonerate Jorgensen's family. Perhaps knowing that his family was all right would make the thought of his death less painful for me. But I also knew I was right. None of them were killers.

"Meet me at the police station?" Ordaz asked. "I'll get you temporarily approved for supervised access to the crime scene. It's helpful to have someone close to the situation on board."

I grabbed my bag and headed for the door. "I'm coming."

The university police station had to be at least a hundred years old. The columned limestone building was covered with ivy and surrounded by towering oak trees. It would've looked more like a library if not for the dozens of police cars in the parking lot.

Inside, the floor, walls, and ceiling were all paneled wood, worn but polished. An older woman sat at the front desk with an open bottle of nail lacquer that she was applying to her fingernails.

"Hello, I'm here to see Detective Ordaz." I put on my most charming face because she seemed like the kind of person who would either love someone or hate them. No in-between. The psychologist in me knew better than to make such snap judgments. But old habits die hard, I suppose.

"Oh." She looked me up and down, then smiled like she was in on some secret. "Well, I'll tell her right away."

The woman stood and walked a few steps down the hallway before calling out, "Sophie, there's a *man* here to see you."

At least she didn't hate me.

Sophie rushed out of her office, her face blazing red with embarrassment. She rolled her eyes at the receptionist.

"Thanks, Gina. This is Dr. Webb. He's helping with the Jorgensen case. Can you please run clearance on him as an informant?" She looked at me apologetically. "She'll just need your I.D. and signature."

"Of course." Gina took my identification but kept the knowing look on her face. She punched a few things into her computer, even though her fingernails were still wet. Then she handed back my card, now smudged with polish. "Here you go, sweetie." She turned to Detective Ordaz. "Looks like he's cleared to help. Not so much as a parking ticket. He's a real keeper."

I nodded at Gina and followed Detective Ordaz back to her office. She sat down in her desk chair. "Not so much as a parking ticket? You a boy scout or something?"

My collar felt suddenly tight, and I tugged on it lightly. "Well, yes. Actually, I was. But that should be irrelevant, right?"

"Maybe." She smiled and shook her head. "Sorry about Gina. She's been here forever and has gotten very comfortable in her job."

"I see that. So, what's your plan, Detective?"

"Well, for now, I'd like you to go meet with the Jorgensen's and see what you can get out of them. Take them some flowers or something, I guess. I'll talk to the folks from your department, and then maybe we'll meet back up and look the office over. Maybe you can tell me if anything looks out of place." She handed me a few twenty-dollar bills. "For the flowers."

"No, thanks." I handed her back the money. "I'll visit them, but only as a sincere friend. If I discover anything suspicious, which I doubt, I'll let you know."

"Have it your way." She shrugged and tucked the money back into her wallet. "I appreciate your integrity. If they really have nothing to hide, then we should clear them as soon as possible. I'd hate to torment the innocent."

"Thank you."

* * *

I pulled up in front of the Jorgensen estate with a large bouquet and a sympathy card. The house had the feel of a college professor's home. Just like the buildings on campus, a decent amount of ivy garnished the worn exterior. The home was red brick and wood, solid and reliable, just like Dr. Jorgensen himself.

A woman I didn't recognize answered the door and let me in. She must've been an aunt or older cousin.

"You said your name's Webb? Let me see if Helen's up to talking to you." She looked at me suspiciously, like she knew I was helping out with the investigation or something.

She led me to a formal living room with leather wingback chairs and sofas. Large pieces of classical art, ornate mirrors, a baby grand piano, and several bookshelves adorned the room. Jorgensen spent endless hours at the university. It was a bit jarring to realize he'd had a life aside from hypotheses, research, and processing data.

A few moments later, Helen Jorgensen joined. She couldn't have been more than fifty years old. Waves of blonde hair fell to her shoulders. Even with her eyes red and swollen from crying, she stood tall and moved gracefully.

"Thank you for stopping by." She looked at me like I'd already overstayed my welcome.

"I'm so sorry for your loss. Walter was a dear friend of mine." I held out the flowers for her. She accepted them but laid them down on the piano without looking at them. "I wondered if there was anything I could do for your family during this time?"

"I don't think so. This has destroyed me. Walter was my everything." A single tear escaped, and she wiped it away quickly. "He was murdered, you know. I can't imagine why anyone would want to hurt him."

"If I find out who's to blame for this, I promise to tell you." I hoped to someday find a wife who cared for me as much as she obviously cared for her husband. She was no murderer. I was sure of that.

"I feel like you know something you're not saying, Doctor." She gestured for me to take a seat, and then she sat on the piano bench, ignoring the chairs and sofa, and rested her elbow on the cover.

"Well, you know we conducted a study on criminal behavior together. A few thoughts have been rolling around in my mind." I sat on one of the wingbacks and rubbed my hand over my face, unsure how much I wanted to share with her at the moment. "I just wonder if maybe he witnessed something, or maybe someone was jealous of him."

"He actually had his car keyed on campus recently. But we don't know who did it, and it's a far cry from murder." Helen rested her head on her hand and looked toward the window. The light of a May afternoon spilled in, leaving a golden halo at the edges of her hair. "I thought maybe you knew something specific. But maybe you know more than you realize."

"It might be worth looking into. The hard thing is sifting out all the things we know and determining which things are important." I shook my head, suspecting that if we weren't all grieving Walter's death, visiting his home would be a delightful experience.

"I know you have a son, Mrs. Jorgensen. How is he doing?" I asked.

"Hank's my stepson. He was devoted to his father. This has utterly devastated him." Her lips turned down into a frown and quivered. "The poor boy."

As if he sensed we were talking about him, the silhouette of a young man appeared in the doorway.

"Come on in, Hank." Helen studied her stepson.

I stepped closer to shake Hank's hand. "Sorry about your dad, I can't imagine what you're feeling. If there's anything I can do?"

We walked back into the room and sat across from Helen.

"Thanks, Henry. I saw him last night, at his office . . ." Hank's voice trailed off.

I knew he didn't hurt his father, but it was clear the family needed lawyers. It appeared that Hank was the last person to see Jorgensen alive.

I phrased my questions carefully, not wanting to spook the kid. "How was he? Anything seem unusual?"

"He was fine. He'd saved me some roast beef and rolls so I could have a sandwich. I worked late, you know?" He shrugged, staring at the ground. His expression reminded me more of a sad child than an impulsive killer. "I wish he would have left when I did."

"Did he say why he stayed late?" I was pushing the boundaries with that question, but it might provide important information.

Hank tensed, then frowned. "Only that he had work to finish. Don't know what could've been so important."

Mrs. Jorgensen cut in, still sniffing. "Hank, you should get some rest."

"I'm so sorry, Mrs. Jorgensen." I stood to hand her a box of tissues, but I didn't return to my seat. "If there is anything at all that I can do for you or your son, please let me know. I feel that I'm intruding on your time."

"I appreciate you coming, Henry." Her face warmed slightly, and I caught a glimpse of the radiant woman from last night. She stood and walked me to the door. "Please be careful. I'm sure someone in the department was responsible for this. I feel it in my gut."

"I'll be careful. Please give the rest of your family my condolences." I nodded and bowed out of the doorway.

As soon as I had the chance, I called Sophie.

"Did you catch any suspects?" She sounded too cheerful for a murder investigator. Perhaps it was her way of detaching from the stress of her job.

"No. His family had nothing to do with his death." I frowned at her.

"You sure?" Now she sounded far too confident for a newbie detective. I wished she would trust my judgment as a psychologist.

Of course, I needed to justify my opinion. "Helen had obviously been crying and seemed heartbroken about losing her husband. She and Hank were nearly in tears. 'Destroyed' was her exact word."

"You talked to Hank?"

"Yes."

"Hmm."

"Helen thinks someone in the department is responsible for this, and I sort of agree with her. But I would suggest taking a closer look at the custodial staff. I'm sure they were all there late, cleaning up." I may have sounded direct, but I didn't feel like she was handling things as professionally as she should. "You have checked the security cameras, right?"

"That's always one of the first things we do. But the cameras only monitor the entrances." She paused, then added. "Of course, I saw that you left way too early to have anything to do with this before I asked for your help."

"Naturally."

She wouldn't be consulting me if I were a suspect.

"It's too bad you don't have a recording from inside." I cleared my throat, not wanting to step on her toes too much. "I'm assuming you checked the cameras from both the main and side entrances?"

"Everyone left long before the professor's time of death. Even Hank, who didn't show up until nine o'clock."

"Aren't there some maintenance doors or something around the back? They're like painted brown metal. Or are those just utilities?" I shouldn't have to be asking these kinds of things.

"There aren't cameras for those. But the staff don't have keys to them either. Only the custodians can use them." She sighed. "That's why I'm hoping you can help us with just one more thing. Then, I'll stop bothering you. Would you be willing to meet me at the crime scene in an hour?"

"I'll be there." But something inside me recoiled. Going back to see the place where Jorgensen was killed wouldn't be pleasant. The morning had been hard enough, and I was beginning to feel the need for some emotional reprieve. No matter how much I wanted to help solve the case, it was personal to me, and I was scared.

Thoughts about my final conversation with Jorgensen swirled in my mind. I wasn't sure how much I wanted to press that line of thinking with the police. Jackson was a good kid and didn't need to be pulled into this any more than Jorgensen's family did.

An hour later, I sat on a bench outside the psychology building, waiting for Detective Ordaz to show up. She pulled up in a squad car and parked in front.

"Thanks for coming. Did they not let you in?" She frowned.

"There's really no point in me going in alone. I think the seventh floor requires a police escort anyway right now." I looked up at the building. It was more modern than the police station, but still had the timeless university feel. It would never be the same for me.

As we headed toward the entrance, I nearly ran into Jackson exiting the building. My mouth fell open for a moment.

The normally enthusiastic blond intern with oversized glasses slumped his shoulder, and he wore a sober expression. "Henry, hi. I guess you heard about Jorgensen? It looks like there's a killer on campus."

"They called you to come here?" I frowned.

"We've been inviting some of the staff to stop by today. It helps if they show us the ins and outs of their general routines." Detective Ordaz spoke flatly, like she wasn't sure she wanted to share the information, and did so against her better judgment.

"I see." Part of me felt sorry for her, she obviously knew she had nothing on anyone and no leads.

Ordaz nudged me away from Jackson and into the building. "You mentioned Jorgensen had some concerns about some paperwork Jackson submitted." She stopped and looked right at me, which made my skin crawl a little.

"I can look into it. But I'm sure it was nothing." I didn't like where this was going. Jackson had his whole life ahead of him, and he'd just lost his internship because Jorgensen died. He didn't need to be accused of murder.

Sophie shrugged. "Can you think of any reason he would've stayed so late last night? He was killed after ten thirty. Would he have been doing research?"

"That's the only reason I can think of for him to have stayed. He was really invested in the recent project because he wanted to make a significant contribution to the field before he died. Unfortunately, our results were inconclusive. For me, it was a small letdown. I've moved on, to be honest." It was heartbreaking to realize Jorgensen would never have the chance to make the difference he'd hoped to, while I still had my whole career ahead of me.

We stepped off the elevator onto the seventh floor. Only one sleepy-looking officer guarded the hall, despite there being several dozen classrooms and offices. He didn't even look at me as we passed—must have thought I was another officer with Sophie.

Our shared office was near the end of the window-lined corridor. The place smelled of books, paper, and the leftover scent of microwavable lunches. The only good thing I could think of was that school had wrapped up for the summer. Having a bunch of undergrad students trying to get up here to meet with professors would have been a nightmare.

"So, I've been digging quite a bit. Of course"—Sophie held open my office door— "I've spoken with Adrianna, who is less than cooperative. She's insisting it must have been a janitor or something because none of you came upstairs last night. But I don't know how she could know that for sure." She scratched her head and walked around my former office. I don't know what I expected the room to be like, but I certainly didn't think everything would be so normal looking.

"I don't see why any of them would've. I would suppose Dr. Jorgensen ran into someone up here and they killed him." There were a few areas around his desk that were blocked off with caution tape. But otherwise, things seemed the same as always. There was no body covered in a sheet or evidence that someone had died in the room last night.

"Jackson's things should be cleared out for the summer," I mumbled, walked over to his desk, and pulled a few drawers open. Nothing inside.

"Yes, his is cleared out for the summer. Looks like you've cleared out most of your stuff as well. Were you planning to take any of those supplies home?" She gestured toward a box of office supplies on my desk.

"No, I thought I'd leave those for whomever replaces me." I shrugged.

"And who will be replacing you?" she asked.

I couldn't see how that mattered one bit. It wasn't me who was murdered. My position was open whether someone killed me or not.

"Well, Jackson, probably—if they keep the spot open now that Jorgensen's gone. Though I doubt he wants to return." I frowned. I wouldn't want to come back after everything.

"Well, the research you were doing was important, wasn't it? Wouldn't you like for it to continue?" She turned and looked directly at me, raising an eyebrow.

"If it were me, I'd start something else. We interviewed a lot of criminals from the prison, processed data. We're trying to see what could've prevented them from breaking the law. But I don't think we've made any breakthrough discoveries." I shook my head. It was a shame, but to some extent, the research we did seemed like a waste of time.

"Really? When I talked to Adrianna about your research. She seemed to think some of your findings had the potential to be rather revolutionary. Maybe you're just humbler about it than you should be." She opened the filing cabinet and pulled out several folders. "I wonder if any of the criminals you interviewed have since been released?"

The entire conversation felt like it was going in the wrong direction. "I doubt any of the criminals we interviewed would have attacked Dr. Jorgensen. We didn't even give them our real names."

I stared at the stack of folders, trying to match the names of the people we interviewed with their faces. There were so many, but I recalled a few. I couldn't see why Sophie was worried about any of these things. Obviously, a crime of passion like what happened to Dr. Jorgensen shouldn't have anything to do with piles of old research.

"I don't know." She stared directly at me again. This was getting uncomfortable. "Maybe it fits. Adrianna verified that there were a bunch of files missing from the cabinet. Someone must have wanted to hide something."

A pit churned in my stomach, and my heart raced. "What are you saying?"

I walked around the desk, inspecting things more closely.

"Only two keys to this cabinet exist. I have Dr. Jorgensen's—but the other was missing. We had our officers serve search warrants to everyone involved in the case this afternoon while you were visiting the Jorgensen's." A smug look crossed her face.

I stepped closer to her. "What'd you find?"

"The other key, and the missing files—in your apartment. It seems like most of the data in the research was falsified, which means your degree is invalid, Dr. Webb." Sophie reached down to the cuffs on her belt.

She was close to the truth.

Too close, and I had to stop her.

I moved quickly, wrapping my hands around her throat before she could respond. This wasn't what I'd planned, but she'd backed me into a corner. It was too bad. She really was a lovely girl. It'd be difficult for her family to work through the loss.

But with the help of a good psychologist, they'd survive.

Her stunned face grew red as she struggled, just like Jorgensen's had last night. I couldn't believe she'd never realized that it would be easy for anyone to steal a custodial key and come back later. The security cameras were pointless.

"It's nothing personal," I whispered in her ear. "I truly doubted you'd figure out what I'd done. It didn't have to end this way."

Sophie struggled against my grip, trying to grab something from her belt.

An ear-splitting crack rang through the air. My head. Searing pain. My vision tunneled and everything went black.

* * *

Detective Sophie Ordaz stood over Henry Webb's lifeless body, trembling. She dropped her gun to the floor just as an officer on duty rushed into the room.

She coughed. Tears streamed down her face. Then she furrowed her brow and anger flashed in her eyes.

"It didn't have to come to this. I thought he'd cooperate, knowing we had evidence against him." Ordaz shook her head. "He underestimated me, I guess—didn't think I could see right through him."

"Have a seat, Detective. You're in shock." The officer, Caleb French, patted her back. "But you were right. This guy wasn't nearly as smart as he pretended to be. Like you said, cheated his way through school, faked his research, and killed the professor who'd discovered the truth. Sad."

Sophie collapsed into Dr. Jorgensen's office chair. "Yeah, he repeatedly insisted that this had been a crime of passion. He was looking for someone to blame but couldn't bring himself to pin it on Jorgensen's son. Of course, we might not have known if Jackson hadn't told us about the inconsistencies in the data. I bet Jorgensen just wanted to ask him a few questions and Webb lost it."

Caleb offered Sophie a water bottle. "Tragic—the university has lost an accomplished professor in Dr. Jorgensen. But we've gained an incredible detective. Congratulations, in less than twenty-four hours, you solved the first case they assigned you."

Police and ambulance sirens blared in the distance.

"I wish I could celebrate. But it feels like such a shame. I doubt Webb realized he was even capable of murder until last night. At least Dr. Jorgensen's family will be able to find closure. I wish I'd realized Webb was a suspect before I sent him over to their house."

"You couldn't have known." Caleb patted her shoulder.

"I know. It's just, once someone has killed someone, I suspect it changes them permanently. Who's to say he wouldn't have tried to hurt the next person who got in his way? He didn't even blink before attempting to kill me." Sophia rubbed her neck.

Caleb looked toward the windows. The flashing police lights were now visible from outside.

Sophie shook her head. "Henry Webb thought he knew everything. The more I witness criminal behavior, human behavior really, the more I realize I still have a lot to learn."

Rebecca Yockey

Rebecca Yockey grew up with two artists for parents, and the freedom to roam the fields and creek near her home. She is an author, editor, and teacher. Her *Magic of the Woods* fantasy series (under Rebecca Avati) is well-loved, and growing. She's an avid mystery reader. When she's not reading or writing, you'll find her teaching math, hanging out with her large family, or painting.

Find out more at www.steamengineproductions.com

8

The Lodemirror Estate

REBECCA YOCKEY

Detective Sophie Ordaz's phone rang, startling her awake. It was twelve-thirty a.m., so pretty much the usual.

"Ordaz, we have a possible murder investigation. Lodemirror Estate just off Alpine Lane. We've got twenty officers here because there are dozens of suspects." Her partner, Caleb French, was already at the scene.

"I know the place." She sat up with her eyes still closed, and pulled them open one at a time. Then she dropped her legs over the side of her bed and flipped on her lamp. She'd have to find another time to catch up on sleep.

Detective Ordaz drove to the side of town where stately houses were separated by expansive yards and mature oak trees lined the streets. In daylight, the area looked like the kind of place where the biggest problems were lost cats, or finding volunteers for the neighborhood fall festival. Families moved there to live out their happily-ever-afters. Finally, the extended gravel driveway of Lodemirror came into view and stopped in front of the imposing limestone mansion nearly

155

overgrown with ivy and oozing with wealth. She took a breath and walked through the front doors.

The house even smelled expensive. The main entry had the same marble checkerboard floors and vaulted ceilings she remembered. It still had the feeling of intentional distance from the modern world. The last time she'd visited the place was as a teenager. Her father had been the mayor, so political hopefuls often invited her family to soirees among the upper crust.

"The body is upstairs, Detective." A uniformed officer started up the grand staircase and looked back to make sure she followed. Sophie picked up her pace, stepping over red plastic cups littering the floor.

The house was over a hundred years old and built at a time when homes were designed to be unique pieces of architecture that reflected their owners' personalities. But the mess indicated that the college kids, who decided to throw a weekend party, had little appreciation for the mansion's history, even though one of them claimed to be the Lodemirror's grandson.

Downstairs, the officers on her team were already busy questioning the partygoers, who insisted they had permission to be there while the Lodemirrors were away. None of the kids claimed to know anything about the woman's death, or that she had even been in the house.

With its stately exterior and classic aesthetic, the home seemed like the type of place where a mystery might occur. At least that's the impression Sophie had as a fifteen-year-old when she attended the gala in her father's honor.

But now, as a homicide detective, it wasn't such an exciting idea to her. It was simply tragic.

Sophie found Officer French in the main corridor upstairs. "Caleb, what can you tell me about the victim?"

He stood in front of an oil portrait of one of the Lodemirrors in a turn-of-the-century suit. "Not much. Here's the deal. An older woman who identified herself as Jeanette Wright had called emergency services saying she saw a dead body in the main bedroom. But in the middle of the call, her phone went dead."

Sophie raised her eyebrows. "So if Jeanette made the call, whose body did they find? And where's Jeanette?"

"That's where things get weird, not that they weren't already. A phone found near the body made the call to dispatch, and we think it belonged to the victim. So far, no one downstairs claimed to know who she was or to have seen anything suspicious. None of them knew anyone besides them was in the house." Caleb led Sophie down the hallway toward the main bedroom.

"You make it sound like Jeanette called in her own murder." Sophie narrowed her eyes. Caleb had always been a little superstitious but he couldn't possibly believe that the ghost of Jeanette made the call.

"Well, that or there's another body somewhere. But she's the only one we've found. Ready to see her?"

Sophie was *never* ready to see a homicide victim. "Ready as I'll ever be."

The body of a sophisticated older woman with perfectly coiffed white hair, wearing a long cream coat, and a pearl necklace, lying amongst the ivory sheets on a massive four-post mahogany bed, with a knife in her chest. She looked like a stage prop.

Chief Ordaz had seen enough bodies that her gag reflex was minimal. But she recognized the familiar churn in her stomach. It would never leave, which she was fine with. It helped her remember that each body was a person who mattered. They had thoughts, ideas, hopes, dreams, and families. It's why she chose her career.

"Poor lady." She shook her head and walked around the room, taking notes. "Who did this to you? And how'd you call in *your own* murder?"

Brick-colored blood splatters soaked the cream-colored duvet, pillows, and carpet. But it didn't look entirely right. Unnaturally bright red globs sat on the white comforter, mixed in with the rest of the gruesome scene. Instinctually she leaned over to smell it.

Ketchup.

She looked more closely at the bed, and just as she suspected, there were obvious thick ketchup blobs mixed in with bloodstains. The woman was deceased, and just recently–probably around eleven p.m., according to her forensics specialist. It might have happened right after Jeanette called dispatch if they had all the times right.

"Any luck getting a second verification of her identity?" Ordaz asked a new officer, as he walked into the room.

"Yes. We scanned her prints into the system. They're a match and the call came from her phone. Unless someone in the house is good at imitating elderly voices, Jeanette Wright somehow called in her own murder." He scratched his head, looking around the room.

Caleb inspected the polished Rococo armoire. "This one's strange, Sophie. The crowd of kids downstairs couldn't have anyone over twenty-three among them."

"Strange is a great word for it. Half of the 'blood' on the bed is actually just ketchup." Sophie yawned. As passionate as she was about solving crime, getting up at one a.m. was horrendous.

"So how many kids are we taking down to the station?" Sophie's mouth tightened. "I suspect most of them are underage."

"That's another weird thing." Caleb's brows pulled together tightly. "No alcohol. They were drinking juice or soda, eating pizza and a ton of spaghetti, playing games, and watching movies. It was an absurdly tame party."

"What?" Sophie ran a hand over her face. "I mean, good for them. But how often do you get forty college kids into a mansion at one a.m. and find them drinking soda?"

"No drugs or anything that we've picked up on, either. Half of them were just watching a movie in the theater room when we arrived." Caleb raised his hands. "Worst crime here, aside from the murder, seems to be the mess they've made. They claim the homeowner's grandson is around here somewhere."

"Alright then, I guess we'll continue with our standard investigation procedures. Keep collecting I.D.s, run background checks on all of the kids, get their stories, and find out who's been hanging out upstairs. Also, ask them why there's no drinking. It's great and all, but I don't get it. We need to find out everything we can about Jeanette Wright."

Sophie Ordaz walked among the groups of college kids on the main floor, who had all cooperated so far. None of them had asked for a lawyer, and most claimed they didn't know why the house was locked down, or that there was a dead body upstairs.

Protocol dictated that officers ask as many questions as possible without offering information that might taint responses. So far, no one said anything about a body.

Sophie found a sleepy-looking kid with white-blonde hair sitting on a tufted Victorian sofa. She might as well start asking questions. "Has anyone interviewed you yet?"

"Nope." He shook his head and lazily handed her his driver's license. "Man, it's getting late."

"It's Friday night. You have important plans in the morning?" She raised an eyebrow.

Annoyance flashed in his eyes. "Well, yeah. Didn't they tell you? We're here carb-loading for the race tomorrow."

"Runners, huh?" Sophie said. That would account for the tame party.

"Half of us are on the men's track team. I was getting ready to leave a couple of hours ago when the police showed up and told us we had to stay." He frowned. He obviously saw the whole thing as a major inconvenience. But it didn't make him look guilty. "I've been trying to nap a little."

"Do you know why we're keeping you all here?" Sophie narrowed her eyes.

"Kat said it could be something about trespassing, but Martin said his grandmother gave him permission to have the team over. He has a key to the house and everything. Some other guy said something about a murder hoax. I don't know." The kid rubbed his forehead and let out a pressured breath. "I can't believe this is happening. We're going to lose tomorrow, that's for sure."

Sophie shook her head, inspecting the kid's license, and wrote his information in her notebook. "Do you know the names of the home-owners? Your name's Zach Jamison, or do you go by Zachary?"

"I think Martin has the same last name as his grandparents, Lodemirror--we're obviously not trespassing." He was leaning back against his chair, eyes closed. "It's just Zach."

"Okay, Just Zach, here's your ID, and you're free to hang out in the movie room. Don't leave though. There's a chance we'll be needing more information from you later."

Zach nodded and rubbed his eyes before getting ready to go. Sophie walked with him to the theater room door where two officers stood on guard. "This one's been questioned. He's good to rest in here."

She made her way back inside and found Officer French interviewing a timid-looking girl with wide brown eyes.

"Anyone come across a Martin or Kat yet?" She asked. "Help spread the word. I don't want either of them trying to leave."

"I haven't, but someone else probably has. We've been taking kids that seem like they may know something to the dining room. Maybe they're there."

Sophie made her way to the dining room, or maybe she should've called it the dining hall. In the center of the room, there was an enormous table that could seat probably twenty people. Ornate benches and credenzas lined the walls and an Austrian crystal chandelier lit the room.

"I'm looking for Martin Lodemirror," she used her official authoritative voice. It didn't come naturally, but she'd gotten better at commanding the attention of an entire room with practice.

A skinny, red-haired distance runner raised his hand. Martin sat leaning back in a dining chair, staring at the ceiling and bouncing his right leg.

"You don't seem too happy." Sophie pulled up a chair next to him at the long table.

"Grandma's gonna kill me. My parents are going to kill me. I was going to clean up the mess and everything, but getting the police called on us. She's gonna..." He lifted both hands and dug his fingers into his mop of red curls.

"Can you confirm your grandparents' names? I'll need all of their contact information." Sophie asked.

"It's just my grandma--she's not here. Grandpa died a few years ago." Martin pulled up his list of contacts on his phone and handed it to Sophie to copy.

Sophie wrote down Mrs. Lodemirror's phone number and email address. "Do you know why the police were called here tonight?"

"I don't know. Did we have too many cars parked on the street?" He looked at her, with fire in his eyes. His jaw was tight, and she wondered if he'd even be willing to speak to her if she wasn't an officer.

"You know this is about more than a few parking violations." Sophie steadied her gaze. She hadn't been a detective for too long. But she could tell when someone was withholding information. They were always more short-tempered or played dumb, and tried way too hard to make direct eye contact.

"Well, I wondered if some of the staff are still here over the week-end. Maybe they thought we didn't have permission to be here." He frowned, shrugging, still staring her in the eyes.

"But, if that were the case, couldn't they have called to check with your grandmother?" Sophie pushed her luck, hoping the kids wouldn't clam up and ask for a lawyer.

"I guess." He rolled his eyes, like a junior high student.

"We're here for a murder investigation, Martin. Since this is your grandmother's home, you're currently our biggest lead. Know anything about that?" He wasn't a suspect by any means, but she had to get him to take the conversation seriously.

Martin's face paled, and he leaned forward in his seat. "What are you talking about?"

"Do you know anyone named Jeanette Wright?" She asked, studying his reaction. She was risking a lot by sharing information with him, but it might be worth it.

"Yeah. She's a rich lady my grandma hangs out with at the country club, I think. Why? Did she kill someone?" He was now leaning completely forward with his elbows on his knees. "She's kind of crazy. I wouldn't be surprised."

"You wouldn't? Tell me why?" Sophie did her best to keep her expression neutral.

"She just seems like she would do anything to keep her money or get even more of it. But she's also really cheap like she's always asking my grandma to buy super expensive things for her. I only know this because my parents talk about it at dinner—like, don't ever act like Ms. Wright, Martin." He raised his hands, shrugging his shoulders.

"Do you know if anyone really hated her, enough to kill her?" Sophie kept the questions coming since the kid was talking. It was risky to share information, but the situation seemed to call for it.

"Wait a second. Are you saying she's dead?" His eyes widened. "Grandma just felt sorry for her, I think. But I've met her. She's really blunt, rude actually, and asks personal questions that she has no business talking about. She'd come over sometimes when I stayed for the weekend–acted like she owned the place."

Sophie nodded, figuring he wouldn't be too traumatized by her questions. And if there were a killer loose in the area, or in the house, he needed to know. It wouldn't be safe to let him stay there if the case wasn't solved within a few hours.

"I'm not a suspect, am I? I've been in the house all night." His anger was melting into panic, which made him look even younger. But at least he was more likely to be forthcoming now, instead of worrying about getting in trouble, or his race.

"I have no reason to believe that you are. But you're not going to want to stay here. Jenette's body is upstairs." Sophie said.

Martin pulled his arms and legs tighter together like he was trying to hug himself. His words barely escaped his mouth. "You think there's a killer in the house?"

"Maybe. But there are over two dozen police officers as well. You're safe for now." She felt sorry for the kid and called an officer over.

"Can you get this kid a blanket and some water? Watch him for shock, but don't let him speak to anyone until I tell you it's okay. He can even lie down on a couch if he wants. I need to contact his grand-mother." Sophie said as she dialed Mrs. Lodemirror's number.

No one answered.

* * *

After asking around, Sophie found Kat in the kitchen, sitting on the floor, dozing with her head leaning back against a cupboard. It looked terribly uncomfortable. She opened her eyes as Sophie sat next to her on the floor.

Kat was maybe twenty years old, with long brown curls, big green eyes, and not too much makeup—seemed pretty well-mannered.

"Hi, Kat. You were telling some people that Martin didn't have permission to have a party tonight. But his grandmother said it was okay. Why were you saying that?"

"I don't know. I just thought maybe there was a misunderstanding." She blinked her eyes open and looked more closely at Sophie. "I didn't want anyone to panic."

"You don't know what's going on?" A twinge of guilt pricked Sophie. She was keeping all these students up late. They were obviously exhausted and likely had nothing to do with the murder.

But then unexpected anger flashed in Kat's eyes. She tightened her lips and shook her head. Sophie's guilt melted away.

"I'll tell you what Kat. If you know something and tell me about it, it's going to be a lot better for you than if you're concealing something during the investigation." Sophie spoke gently, not wanting to spook her--good cop and all that.

"I don't know anything about your murder investigation." Kat tightened.

"I didn't say anything about murder, Kat." Sophie reached down to her side, ready to pull out her handcuffs.

Fear rushed over Kat's face. "It was just a joke, seriously. I mean, like, with ketchup and stuff. I'm really sorry, but no one got hurt."

"Now we're getting somewhere." Sophie nodded, scribbling in her notebook. "If you'll tell me all about that, I'd appreciate it. If it really was just a joke, you shouldn't have anything to worry about."

"My aunt Jeanette has been pushing me to date Martin. I think she wants me to marry him for his money or something. But Martin is just a friend—no chemistry, whatsoever. So I came up with this idea, and it sounds really dumb now that I'm saying it out loud to a cop." She paused for a minute to look at Sophie like she was trying to decide whether she could trust her. "Me and Martin and a few of our friends decided that if we set up a fake murder scene in the house and said that his family was in the mob or something, she would stop hounding me. I mean, it would've been funny. She's been butting into everyone's business for years and just needed to be put in her place."

"Did you use a bunch of ketchup?" Sophie asked.

"Well, yeah. We put some old sheets in the main bedroom and I invited my aunt to stop by. I told her Martin's grandma wanted her to come over to give her something. I showed her up to the bedroom. Martin didn't come to help me show her the 'body' because we wanted her to be suspicious of him as well. We had our friend Ashton lying on the bed, all covered in ketchup. I told her that the family was connected to the mob, and we needed to not get involved. But she didn't agree with me, freaked out, ran to the bathroom, and locked the door."

"What time did this happen?" Sophie put the pieces together in her mind and continued to maintain a calm demeanor, in hopes that Kat would keep talking.

"It was probably like ten or something. I'm not sure." Kat nervously twisted her brown curls in her fingers.

"I knocked on the door and told her to get out of the bathroom and that we should just leave. But she yelled at me and accused me of being in on 'the murder.' I guess I should have told her it was a joke. But she was taking it seriously, which was kind of good. I went downstairs to find Martin because I decided I should let him know she was freaking out, and..." Kat's words trailed off and her bottom lip began trembling. Tears spilled from her eyes.

Sophie found a clean kitchen towel and handed it to Kat, then patted her back. "It's okay. Take all the time you need."

After a few minutes, Kat pulled in a deep, shuddering breath and wiped her tears. "I'm okay. I just didn't realize faking a murder was a crime. Anyway, it took forever to find Martin. The house is huge and there were so many people here. I finally found him in here, trying to cook more pasta for everyone on the track team. This was a carb-loading party, kind of. I mean, a bunch of us just came for fun. I personally think running for fun is absurd."

"So you were saying something about Martin? What happened next?" Sophie hoped this girl hadn't gone back up and murdered her aunt. She hated the idea of having some kid spending the rest of their life in prison.

"Yeah, I told him. He just looked at me, really confused, like he didn't understand what I was talking about. I probably didn't explain it very well. But before he could really say anything we heard all these really loud police cars outside and he ran to see what was going on."

It dawned on Sophie that Kat might not even know her aunt had died. "Did you see your aunt after you'd left her in the bathroom?"

"Well, no. The police came barging in and made us stay here. I bet she was the one that called, right? I'm going to be in so much trouble." Kat's eyes filled with tears. "I don't know if I can get into medical school if I have a criminal record."

"Kat." Sophie needed more information, so she pushed further. "We're not here investigating a murder hoax. Your aunt Jeanette is dead."

Kat blinked several times and narrowed her eyes at Sophie. She barely whispered. "What are you talking about?"

"You sure you haven't been upstairs since you left your aunt in the bathroom?" Sophie asked.

"What? Of course not, I didn't do anything." Kat's voice grew shrill, and her eyes were wide like baseballs. She breathed heavily. "My parents are going to kill me. Oh...I didn't mean that..."

"Breathe, Kat. Try to calm your body. You're not under arrest at this time. I need you to stay here, with these officers for the time being. Can you point out Ashton to me?" It was far too early to make any assumptions about who did what, but Sophie wanted to keep her people of interest as calm and coherent as possible.

Ashton was in the theater room with the other kids who'd already spoken with an officer. He sat in a corner, wearing a sweatshirt with a hood pulled up over his head. He folded his arms tightly across his chest, clearly not interested in talking to anyone.

"You're Ashton, right?" she asked.

"Yeah." He nodded.

"It's pretty warm in here. But you still want to wear that big old hoodie?" Sophie asked.

His eyes widened. "Do I need a lawyer or something?"

"That's up to you. You're not under arrest." Sophie pulled up a chair near him. Being at eye level instead of standing over him would be less intimidating. Though he'd probably tower over her by a foot or so if he stood.

"Did Kat tell you about the joke? What do you know?"

"She told me. But I want to hear your side of things. What'd you see, Ashton?"

Ashton was quiet, staring at the floor for a minute. "Nothing."

"Nothing?"

"Well, yeah. I was lying on the bed. My eyes were closed. They come in. Kat's a talented actor because she sounded surprised to find me there and started going on about how the family had connections to the mob. It was kinda funny." He tightened his lips and nodded.

"It seems like a weird trick to play on someone, you know? Why not just tell her aunt to stop bothering her?" Sophie said. There was obviously a missing piece in all of this. So far, the situation was odd, but nothing she'd heard sounded like a motivation for murder.

"You don't get it. Her aunt is completely crazy. Trying to set any boundaries with her is impossible. She is just toxic, like textbook narcissism. But it wasn't just that. She will take everything she can from people. We don't know where she gets her money, but she doesn't have a job or anything and her husband couldn't have left her with much when he died. Kat's terrified of her." Ashton's upper lip turned up in disgust.

"Terrified? Did you see what happened when she came out of the bathroom?" Sophie asked.

"Nah. Of course, the whole thing backfired. I left when Kat did. It was a stupid prank." He shook his head. "Now the police are here, freaking everyone out. For what?"

Something about Ashton's tone made Sophie inclined to believe his innocence. He was too annoyed with the situation to be guilty. If he'd done anything, he'd probably be acting as helpful as possible, but there would be fear in his eyes. That had been her experience with killers in the past, anyway.

She didn't think Ashton needed to know anything else. "Well, hopefully, we'll get you all out of here quickly. I'm glad you were only covered in ketchup."

"Well, tomato sauce, but it's all the same." Ashton shrugged.

"Thanks, Ashton." That was the missing piece she'd been looking for. She stood and hurried from the theater, back toward the dining room.

"Where's the kid I had Officer Harris looking after?" Sophie asked another officer.

"Oh, he had to use the restroom, I think. Down that hall." The officer pointed her in the right direction, and Sophie scurried down the hall to find Officer Harris standing outside a door.

"Martin's in there, right? Have you been here long?" She asked him.

"It's been at least five minutes." Officer Harris pounded on the door with the back of his hand. "Hey kid, you alright in there?"

No answer.

"Hey Martin, we're getting worried. I'm opening the door in three, two, one." She and Officer Harris pounded into the door and it burst open. The room was empty and a window near the bathtub was wide open.

She pulled out her walkie. "We've got a suspect. Martin Lodemirror. He's a student, with lots of curly red hair, left through a bathroom window approximately five minutes ago. Keep the other students where they are. Those that are available to help: search the perimeter."

A flurry of motion picked up around the home, officers shouting into walkies, running down halls. They should be able to find him soon. Sophie decided the best course of action was to climb out the bathroom window herself and see if she could trace Martin's movements.

His footprints were easy to follow through the flower garden surrounding the house and led in the direction of a greenhouse. Thoughts flew through Sophie's mind as she tore down the path.

It looked like Martin was guilty. He was evading the police, after all. But it was difficult to imagine that he'd planned such a sloppy crime. And even though Martin expressed obvious disdain for Jeanette Wright, he hardly had a motivation for murder.

Sophie slowed her pace as she approached the greenhouse doors. A faint light flickered inside—probably from a cell phone.

As silently as possible Sophie pushed open a door. She pulled out her gun and mag light, even though she had no intention of shooting anyone.

The substantial building was filled with long rows of plants preparing for the upcoming season. Musty and heavily scented with a mix of floral and herbal plants, the air seemed to slow Sophie down. She paused to calm and quiet her breathing. "Martin, it's Detective Ordaz. I'm armed and need you to come out nice and steady—hands where I can see 'em."

"You shouldn't come in here." Martin's voice sounded more concerned than afraid. "You're not safe."

Sophie furrowed her brows, scanning the darkness for whatever threat had him on edge. "We just need you to come back to the house, Martin. All we need to do is talk, get some information, and make sure your grandma is safe to come back home."

"Please." He sounded more like a child begging to get his way than a college student. "Just leave me alone. I didn't stab that old lady. It wasn't me."

"I don't remember telling you how she died, Martin." Sophie's brain spun with possibilities. He could be covering for someone, or for himself. It was possible that Jeanette Wright had attacked him first and it was self-defense. She trod forward, nearly tripping over a garden hose.

A shadow darted behind Sophie. A flower pot flew toward her, crashing into her shoulder and knocking her to the ground. Her vision blurred and splintering pain shot down her arm, nearly making her drop her gun.

"Stop!" Martin shouted from across the building. The silhouette standing over Sophie, ready to pummel her with another pot, belonged to an older woman in a long coat.

"Jeanette?" Sophie blinked, dodging a terracotta plant slamming into the ground, narrowly missing her head, shattering, and spraying dirt into her face. She rolled over, panting, and pushed herself to her feet, pointing her weapon at her assailant.

"You'll stay out of our lives if you know what's best for you." The older woman shrieked.

Our lives? As in her's and Martin's?

The case clarified in Sophie's mind. "Hands up Mrs. Lodemirror."

The elderly woman turned and ran toward the door, but she grunted as she crashed into someone. Sophie flashed her light at the scuffling pair to catch glimpses of Martin restraining his grandmother.

In a flash Sophie cuffed Mrs. Lodemirror, ending the struggle. She repeated the usual dialogue. "You're under arrest. You have the right to remain silent…"

Martin whimpered. "Seriously, grandma. I don't know what Jeanette had on you, but it wasn't worth killing her over."

"But now our family is free of her forever." A wicked sigh of relief spread over Mrs. Lodemirror's face. "No one can ever take what is rightfully yours, my sweet Martin."

* * *

A week after the Lodemirror case, Sophie sat at her desk rubbing a knot in her shoulder. Caleb knocked on the doorframe as he let himself into her office.

"Ibuprofen and caffeine—been using that combo for years to take care of my back." His laugh was too sad to be funny.

"We any closer to a motive on the Lodemirror case?" Sophie gave up trying to put together any clues in the robbery case she was reviewing and looked away from her computer.

"The lady still won't talk, but the kid and his parents think Jeanette Wright was blackmailing Mrs.Lodemirror, claiming to be an "illegitimate" half-sister and heir to the estate. Don't you think using the word illegitimate to describe someone is awful?" He shrugged, but Sophie got the feeling that he bought that story.

"Yep, I do. So why'd the kid crawl out of the bathroom window?" Sophie smirked.

Caleb shrugged. "Sounds like he witnessed the murder, or saw his grandmother sneaking out of the house. He says they told her about the prank they were going to play because of the pressure on Kat. His grandmother must have decided to take matters into her own hands. I guess they're still working on clarifying everyone's statements though."

"It does make some sense. Though if Jeanette really was related to the Lodemirrors, she had some awful ideas. I mean, Jeanette was trying to set up her niece, Kat, with Martin. Unbelievable what people will do to get their hands on money." Determination set into Sophie's heart. Accepting the world as it was, where people sometimes thought horrendous acts were solutions to problems didn't sit well with her. "Lodemirror won't get away with this. People need to know that no one is above the law, no matter what they feel their social status is."

"Ah, there's your fierce sense of justice. Some people will do anything for money. On the other hand, some–ahem, cops–work their tails off for barely livable wages because it gives them a sense of purpose."

Caleb smiled with half of his mouth and shook his head. "Maybe we're the crazy ones."

Sophie laughed to herself. "We'll never become wealthy doing this, but we're being *richly rewarded* with meaningful work—and knots in our shoulders."

"Yep. Living the dream." Caleb rolled his eyes, and he walked out of her office as unceremoniously as he'd entered.

"Living the dream," Sophie whispered, thinking of the questions she had about her own past. Something always seemed off with the Lodemirrors, even back when her father was mayor. "Or at least I might be seeing things more clearly."

Rebecca Yockey

Rebecca Yockey grew up with two artists for parents, and the freedom to roam the fields and creek near her home. She is an author, editor, and teacher. Her *Magic of the Woods* fantasy series (under Rebecca Avati) is well-loved, and growing. She's an avid mystery reader. When she's not reading or writing, you'll find her teaching math, hanging out with her large family, or painting.

Find out more at www.steamengineproductions.com